C000131539

CYBORG FEVER

INTERSTELLAR BRIDES® PROGRAM: THE COLONY - 5

GRACE GOODWIN

Cyborg Fever: Copyright © 2018
by Grace Goodwin
Interstellar Brides® is a registered trademark
of KSA Publishing Consultants Inc.
All Rights Reserved. No part of this book may be reproduced or
transmitted in any form or by any means, electrical, digital or
mechanical including but not limited to photocopying, recording,
scanning or by any type of data storage and retrieval system without
express, written permission from the author.

Published by KSA Publishers
Goodwin, Grace
Cyborg Fever, Interstellar Brides® Program: The Colony - 5

Cover Copyright © 2019 by Grace Goodwin
Images/Photo Credit: Deposit Photos: fxquadro, Angela_Harburn

Publisher's Note:
This book was written for an adult audience. The book may contain
explicit sexual content. Sexual activities included in this book are strictly
fantasies intended for adults and any activities or risks taken by fictional
characters within the story are neither endorsed nor encouraged by the
author or publisher.

GET A FREE BOOK!

JOIN MY MAILING LIST TO BE THE FIRST TO KNOW OF NEW RELEASES, FREE BOOKS, SPECIAL PRICES AND OTHER AUTHOR GIVEAWAYS.

http://freescifiromance.com

INTERSTELLAR BRIDES® PROGRAM

YOUR mate is out there. Take the test today and discover your perfect match. Are you ready for a sexy alien mate (or two)?

VOLUNTEER NOW!
interstellarbridesprogram.com

1

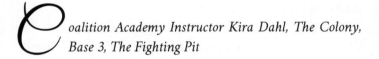

oalition Academy Instructor Kira Dahl, The Colony, Base 3, The Fighting Pit

"I SEE THE WAY YOU'RE PANTING AFTER HIM. I DON'T BLAME you; that Atlan is so damned hot." Hearing the words come out in my friend's cute German accent almost made me burst into laughter. Years of discipline saved me.

I turned and glared at Melody, gave her my infamous instructor narrowed-eyes look. Actually, it was my *Don't-Fuck-With-Me* cop face, but she didn't know that. It had worked pretty well on the streets of Toronto, but Melody was a friend, and apparently, unaffected by my hard-won glare.

She glanced from the Atlan Warlord, who was about to fight in the pit, to me, giving me that all-too familiar sweet and innocent look. "What? Don't tell me I'm wrong. You're eyeing him like an all-you-can-eat dessert buffet back home."

I turned back to the scene before us, pursing my lips and hoping my cheeks weren't turning bright red. While I refused to admit it, my Earth friend—and senior cadet— was right. The Atlan *was* one fine male specimen. Tall, dark and handsome wasn't enough to do him justice. He had to be close to seven feet tall with a physique that made me think he ate Crossfitters back home for breakfast. But since he was standing—shirt off, I might add—in a fighting pit, he had the hard edges, the cut muscles, of a male who'd survived ruthless action. Battle. Devastation. He was scarred, and those scars made me hot. So freaking hot. I wanted to trace every single one of them with my tongue.

He had cyborg parts like the rest of them on The Colony—both of his arms were covered in the shining silver of circuitry and muscle implants. He had a thick scar on the back of his neck, but I had no idea if that was from the Hive or something that had happened in battle. After almost a year of bringing recruits to The Colony for training, I was used to seeing the silver parts of the warriors who lived here. I was no longer surprised when a fighter had glistening metal embedded in his flesh. The implants meant nothing to me except as badges of honor. He'd battled the Hive, fought hard, survived. Everyone on this planet had and I respected every single warrior here.

But this Atlan made my body go on red alert. I couldn't see his legs, as they were covered by pants, but his back and chest were bare. Hot muscular perfection that I wanted to touch. And lick. And pet. And kiss.

My body hummed with a surprising need. My libido had gone into hibernation in recent times; as an instructor, there was no fraternizing with the cadets at the Coalition Academy, even if I was only a few years older than most of the new recruits. Abstaining hadn't been a problem. And since the other instructors and administrators didn't push any of my buttons, it made my no-men, no entanglements rule pretty easy to follow. But looking at the Atlan, I licked my lips. Rule or no rule, I wanted a piece of that.

"If that's him normally, I wonder what he looks like in beast mode," she added, leaning in and murmuring in my ear. She pointed at the way the Atlan paced, eyeing his foe from the edge of the fighting area, clenching his hands open and closed into fists. That only corded the muscles and tendons in his forearms. Holy shit. Him in beast mode? Bigger, bulkier, more dominant. Intense. Ruthless.

My pussy was yelling at me, *yes, please!* And the fighting hadn't even begun yet. It was...elemental, this interest I had in him. Visceral. I didn't know his name, his life story. He hadn't even taken me to a dinner and a movie and yet I wanted him. Instant attraction. This was not like what I'd been told about the Everians and their Marked Mates. Nothing so intense that I couldn't walk away and be able to function. But one Everian cadet had left mid-term because his mark had awakened, and he'd lost focus or interest in anything but tracking her down and claiming her.

What I wanted with this very large piece of man candy was a...one-night-stand kind of thing. Hot and hard. Fast and primal. I was so bad, but everything in me was screaming at me to strip naked and jump him. Name. No name? My pussy didn't care. I wanted a man-made orgasm and my body had decided this Atlan Warlord was the one to give it to me.

His opponent, from the caramel coloring and sharper facial features, was a Prillon. He paced on the far side of the pit talking with a few others, most likely discussing strategy. He was smaller, but that only meant he was well over six feet. Two huge aliens were about to face off in the well-known pit. By the size of the crowd watching from the seats that formed a semi-circle around the fighting area, it was an off-duty pastime. The buzz, the hum that came from everyone was heady. Everyone we'd met on this planet was intense, their pasts with the Hive certainly setting the tone. The fighters had rage and pain to release and the fighting pits—even if they were just watching—was an outlet for that.

"You know what they say," Melody began. "That the size of his hands is indicative of the size of his—"

I laughed as I put a hand over her mouth, stifling the rest of that sentence. She waggled her eyebrows. So much for my well-practiced intimidation face.

"Okay, enough!"

She and my pussy were telling me one thing—jump the giant—my brain, another.

She pursed her lips together, but I could tell she was dying to say more. Our friendship went far beyond instructor/cadet. We were both from Earth, the only two in this year's academy. While she was from Germany and I was from Canada, we had so much in common. Especially being a galaxy away from home. She was almost finished with her training at the Coalition Academy and would move on to an official fighting assignment upon graduation. I was an instructor there; the youngest the Academy had ever had. Because of my age, I had more in common with the cadets than with the other teachers.

And Melody? She was a riot and I adored her. Except for right now. It wasn't often she could poke fun at me— we didn't have tons of downtime when I wasn't her instructor and there were rank protocols to follow then— and she was enjoying herself. Immensely.

It was also rare that we weren't on Zioria. Off-planet training missions occurred in the last few weeks of a term, and only with those about to graduate. It was our last chance to run full-scale battle simulations and try to prepare them for what was coming. There were a few other human instructors, most of them ex-military or CIA. Strategy. Weapons. We called the young, aggressive, naïve recruits *zygotes*. Babies. All of them. From every world. They had no idea what they were getting into.

We did. We knew what was out there. I'd been with the Intelligence Core for over three years now, the Coalition Academy teaching position my cover for sensitive operations. But I had a job to do with these recruits, and I took it seriously. The better we did our job training them, the fewer had to die.

That was why we were all on The Colony, doing mission simulations with this term's graduates. But those were completed, and now we had a night for the group to relax. For *me* to relax.

Or fuck an Atlan.

"He is hot," I offered, then bit my lip. When she rolled her eyes, I added, "Fine. He's absolutely gorgeous if you like that dark, brooding giant type." I sighed. "Which I do." *Oh, I so do.*

"There are no rules against getting it on with a hot Atlan beast," she replied.

"We're here on The Colony for cave training," I reminded her. My specialty was stealth training. Get in, get out, don't get caught. As far as the warriors knew, if they were captured by the Hive, it was over. No one was coming for them. And ninety-nine percent of the time, that was true. But for the other one percent, there was the I.C.—the Intelligence Core. In teams of two or three, we went in and recovered high level targets.

It was dangerous, but important work. The Hive couldn't be allowed to break open the mind of an I.C. team member. We knew too much. About everything.

Two fighters walked along our row and we stood to let them pass, both of them huge Prillon warriors. They looked at us like we were candy and sat not too far away, on my left.

Testosterone overload. Too many hot warriors. We were literally surrounded.

The Prillon duo stared, made sure I knew they were interested. But I only had eyes for one warrior at the moment. And he was magnificent. My entire body went into heat at the sight of him. God, that Atlan was fucking *hot*. I'd only run into an Atlan a couple of times. They kept to themselves at the Academy, their instructors huge Atlan warriors themselves just in case one of them lost control of his beast during training.

Their women didn't go into beast mode and didn't fight in the Coalition, which I refused to have an opinion on. I knew their males were big, protective, dominant —big.

The shiver that raced through my body had nothing to do with the Prillon warriors scooting closer, and everything to do with the play of shadows over the Atlan fighter's abs. I wanted to lick him there, make my way down…

"Training's been over for two hours," Melody was talking. Why was she still talking?

She sat back down and prattled on, oblivious to the Prillon warriors and their obvious interest. "You're the one who dismissed us all and told us to have some fun for our last night on the planet. Our transport back to the Academy isn't scheduled until tomorrow. You have *all* night." She leaned toward me, bumped her shoulder into mine.

More spectators filled the stands until it was practically overflowing. They all wore the uniform of their position and rank prior to arriving on The Colony. Every warrior was covered in light-weight battle armor, most camouflaged black and grey for deep space battle. Melody and I were the only ones in Academy uniforms, hers gray, mine black, indicating my role as instructor.

"I'm not looking for a mate." Absolutely not. Men complicated everything. They were selfish. Controlling. Difficult. Assholes. At least the ones I'd tangled with on Earth. Because of that, I'd avoided the ones in space, even the alien hotties that had crossed my path working for the Academy and my side stint in the I.C. The warriors in the I.C. weren't selfish, but they were definitely controlling, dominant and would be difficult to deal with in an intimate relationship.

I didn't need a man telling me what I could or could not do. I was not ready to settle down and be a baby

7

machine for an alien when there were people out there who needed me, people I could save.

The way I hadn't been able to save my parents.

"Who said anything about a mate? I thought we were talking about hot sex here, sister. And he's practically *screaming* with hotness."

"If I wanted a mate, I'd have joined the Interstellar Brides Program," I added, making it blatantly clear my stance.

"Okay, but you *have* had a fling before? Back on Earth? At least one?"

I offered her a shrug in response. Earth was behind me. What I'd done there was irrelevant to my life now. Although I could say I'd never seen such a fine specimen of the XY chromosome on display as in the fighting Atlan.

All at once the crowd cheered, many stood, some put their hands to their mouths and shouted. The two fighters in the pit began to pace back and forth. I didn't know how this fighting thing worked here, what the rules were. There was no ring, no ropes, no corner stool. There weren't mouth guards or headgear either. No referee.

"Well?" Melody asked, and I remembered her original question.

"Yes, I had a couple one-night stands," I replied, as if I was weird if I hadn't. "Nothing all that wild."

She laughed and pointed at the Atlan who was moving to the center of the pit. "That's because there is nothing as wild as him back on Earth." Her hand came up and she fanned herself.

No, there wasn't.

The two fighters kept their distance, about five feet between them, as they circled. I could see the play of muscle across the Atlan's back, the way his shoulders bunched and relaxed as his arms moved in front of him. Even with their size and heft, their feet were quiet on the packed earth. These weren't newbies at the Academy, fresh faced and eager to prove how brilliant and ruthless they supposedly were. No, these two had met the Hive personally, seen too much and were most likely jaded, dark edged and ruthless.

The Prillon warrior was handsome, in his own way. Big. Muscular. Focused. But I barely noticed him. I couldn't take my eyes off the Atlan.

Based on my Coalition training, I knew they were sizing each other up, discovering their dominant stance and other tells. They spoke to one another, their low, baritone voices making my pussy clench in heat. His voice. God. I leaned forward, trying to hear their words. The threats. The challenge.

I wasn't normally one to *enjoy* violence, but I had to hit my thighs with fists to keep myself from standing, from yelling at the Atlan to *end him.* I knew my Atlan was going to be impressive. His size. His strength. The intensity in his eyes. I wanted him to be powerful. I needed him to be magnificent. The need was shocking, but pounding through my blood like a low level electrical current. Like a pulse. And I couldn't look away.

I held my breath and waited for the first strike. This was going to be quite a match.

The Atlan came about so he faced us once again. His eyes were on his opponent, laser sharp. His left leg was forward, his left hand up, open handed, his right lower and guarding his center.

"Yes! Go, go go! Do it!" The words exploded out of me

with a violence that was shocking. I wanted to hear the strike of his fist on the Prillon's flesh. I suspected I was losing my mind a bit, maybe overreacting because of all the stress I'd been under the last few months, but I felt wild. Totally out of control. I *needed* the satisfaction of watching my Atlan pound his opponent into dust.

My pussy wanted it too, so hot and wet I was throbbing with need, like this was foreplay, not a pit fight on what amounted to an alien prison colony.

For some reason, he glanced away, into the stands. He smiled, said something to the other fighter. I didn't have to hear the words to know it was a taunt and I wished I could hear what he'd said. Right or wrong, I knew it would turn me on.

Once again, he looked to the audience, this time though, his eyes met mine.

Held.

My heart skipped a beat. It was that weird feeling, like riding in a car and going over a rise, the plummeting sensation that makes one's skin hot, sweat breaking out on a cool brow.

"Holy shit," Melody mumbled. I felt her grip my elbow, dig her fingers in, but I didn't turn my head. I couldn't.

Those dark eyes looked at me. *Saw* me. Held me pinned in place. My breath was trapped in my lungs. My breasts were heavy and hot and I couldn't move.

"Um, Dahl. He's looking at you."

No shit.

The Atlan, seemingly brought out of his stupor over me—which was ridiculous because I was far from exciting in my plain uniform, my hair pulled back in the usual low ponytail—began to move again, doing that circling thing once more, but he continued to watch me.

Me!

"He's going to get knocked out if he doesn't focus on the match," I murmured. I bit my lip, suddenly worried for the big guy. Distraction was *not* what he needed at the moment.

My ovaries liked that I was his distraction though. My pussy clenched, my nipples got hard from the way he was watching me. God, it was powerful. Was this what the Everians felt like when their marks awakened?

No, this wasn't like that. I didn't feel it in my soul. *This* I felt in all my female parts. Every single one of them. This was pure lust. I was aroused by him. Seriously turned on. I wanted him. Not to keep, but to make this ache go away. And if he was as big *everywhere* as Melody had been joking about, then it would be an amazing ride.

I did have twelve hours free and clear of my duties. No teaching, no missions for the I.C. Nothing but downtime where I could relieve this ache that was growing by the second. And I wanted the Atlan to take care of it for me.

If he didn't end up in the med unit first.

The Prillon let out a bellow and attacked. I sucked in a breath as he charged, fists at the ready. The Atlan didn't look away from me until the Prillon landed a punch. I grimaced at the sound of the two brutes colliding, but the Atlan barely seemed to notice the attack. Lightning fast, he retaliated.

The crunching sound of bone breaking could be heard over the din of the crowd. Blood spurted from the Prillon's nose as he fell, like a redwood in the forest, to the ground. His arms didn't go up to stop his fall, indicating he'd been knocked unconscious immediately.

One punch. That was all it took. The fight was over.

The Atlan took a deep breath, let it out, and I watched the ripple of his eight-pack abs as he did so. He gave the Prillon a quick look, glanced at the medical team, who was already running toward the fallen warrior, then looked back at me.

He strode across the pit and to the edge of the stands, straight toward me, like we were connected by a wire.

The crowd parted like the Red Sea before Moses and they turned to see what held the Atlan's attention. Behind him, the Prillon was being assisted and I could see he was coming to, his blood staining the dirt. His jaw at an awkward angle, obviously broken.

Ouch.

"Um, Dahl, he's *really* staring at you."

I glanced at the others who had come to watch the fights and they were all looking at me, too.

When I looked back at the Atlan, he had his hand up and he curled his finger. Beckoning me.

I gulped. Swallowed. Was he really talking to me?

I looked around. Everyone was watching me, waiting to see what I would do.

Oh, shit. All me. I wasn't imagining things.

Melody pushed me and I stumbled forward. "Go, woman!"

I stepped down a row, closer to him, glanced back at Melody. She had a sly smile on her face. "Don't do anything I wouldn't do. Well, no, do a whole bunch of things I wouldn't do." She nodded her head, giving me some kind of reassurance for going after the Atlan.

I licked my lips, looked at the Atlan again. Oh yeah, I wanted him and he *obviously* wanted me.

His skin had a slick sheen of sweat that only highlighted each and every one of his rippling muscles. He turned his hand over, palm up, saying without words that I should take it.

I went down the rows, one after the other until I stood before him. He was so damned big, well over a foot taller than I was, closer to two.

Pheromones must be pumping from him because all I wanted to do was lick his neck and taste his salty skin. Run my palms over his torso and lower to the button on his pants. To grip his cock, stroke it. Rule him.

I wanted to *own* him. Pet him. Ride him. I wanted him, all of him, just for me. Filling me up. Making me beg. Making me come all over his huge—

His fingers came up, stroked over my cheek and I held my breath. The feel of the gentle caress was unnerving and surprising considering his size.

"Mine," he said, his voice loud, as if he were telling everyone who could hear that I was off the market. I thought of the crestfallen looks that were probably gracing the faces of the two Prillon warriors behind me and stifled a smile.

For now, for tonight, he was all mine.

So I put my hand in his, ready to spend a wild night with an Atlan—and hopefully, his beast.

2

*W*arlord Anghar, The Colony

MY BEAST WAS RAGING. THE PRILLON STANDING ACROSS from me in the fighting pit had not chosen a second to fight beside him. Either the poor bastard was an idiot, or this stubborn Prillon hadn't been in The Colony long enough to choose one.

I would place a wager on the second. I saw the need in his eyes. The need to rage.

To hurt.

He wanted to come at me. To fight. To hold nothing back. I knew that feeling, that desperate, clawing need to punch, kick. Beat.

To hurt. To bleed. To feel something real.

I missed the rush of battle, the elation of victory. When we fought the Hive, we were important to the Coalition. Protecting others. Doing important work.

Now? We mined for the transport system. We counted the days and fought off boredom with every waking breath. Irrelevance. We were nothing now, and that was like swallowing a blade. It hurt, all the way through.

"I'm going to make you bleed, Warlord." The Prillon was panting, eager to get the fight started. His hands were in fists at his sides, his chest thick and well-muscled. Anger and anticipation simmered.

I welcomed the challenge. The distraction. The only thing I wanted more than to spend a couple hours in this fighting pit was a warm, wet pussy. A mate begging me to fuck her. Taste her. Fill her with my seed. My beast prowled within me at that thought.

But there was no bride for me. Never would be. I'd taken the bride testing more than long ago with no success. I happened to believe the ban on brides for contaminated warriors was a valid one. We were not whole. Never would be. Not that my opinion mattered. Most of the warriors here had submitted to the Interstellar Brides Program testing protocols when Prime Nial lifted the ban for Colony exiles more than a year ago. And we could count the brides that had arrived at Base 3 on one hand.

Just because he'd allowed the contaminated to be matched didn't mean there was hope for any of us.

Brides were few and far between here. Some said their presence gave the other warriors hope. But I'd always been a realist. There would be no saving me. No soft, beautiful female deserved the monster I carried within. He was too feral. I doubted even the legendary Atlan mating cuffs would affect him, would soothe the animal within.

The Hive had taken too much. Forced me into beast mode and tortured me for days. In the end, they had broken me, and my beast, and I still carried the shame.

I should have made them kill me. And when Seth Mills had the chance, he hadn't done it either, taking away the quiet of death. And now I lived. And fought. Not for life or death, not against the Hive that still stalked us all, but in a round pit on a desolate world with other fucked-up and exiled warriors. Not to save people, but for a break from the monotony of this new existence.

If I wasn't such a bastard, I'd end it. But despite all the rambling that went on in my head, I was a survivor. Always had been. Hope or no hope, I'd hold on until the bitter end, until my beast raged and they were forced to execute me. I was too stubborn to die.

"Fucking Atlan. What are you waiting for?" The Prillon was pacing me. Circling. His gaze filled with horror and rage and hatred, all directed at himself. We were one in that moment, and I knew my gaze matched his. Broken. We were both broken.

"You can't beat me, Prillon. But you already know that, don't you? That's not why you're here." I threw the taunt, knowing it for truth. He *wanted* to feel the pain. To attack with nothing held back. He couldn't kill me. Not without a second Prillon warrior to back him up. And I wouldn't kill him. He was a warrior, an honorable soldier who'd survived the same horrors I had. Death matches were not allowed in the pit, so fighting me was the closest he could get. But I could make him hurt. Bleed.

Feel.

Two more steps. Three. Screaming voices fueled us both, but there was one sound that drew my beast's attention away from the match and my gaze lifted to scan the crowd before I had processed the instinct. I never looked away from an opponent in the pit. It was a rookie move. A stupid one. But I had no choice. My beast forced my hand.

It was a woman's voice. A female.

My beast awoke, practically howled as fire rolled through my veins and my cock grew hard.

I shook my head, trying to blink away the urge to hunt down that voice. To claim her.

She was probably one of the Academy cadets here for training but leaving tomorrow.

I should ignore it. Let her go. She wasn't my matched mate. Couldn't be.

I didn't have one.

Another reason my beast was so edgy. There seemed little hope I'd be able to hold on long enough to discover a mate that my beast would want to claim. Of the warriors here, only Warlord Braun understood the monster inside me, raging to break free. Every moment was an act of discipline. Every step. Every breath. The beast seethed, and I held him down with an iron fist, my will the only thing standing between me and execution.

The fighting pits helped release some of the beast's restlessness, the *hunger*. But my time as a Hive drone hadn't dimmed the beast's fury, as it had with Warlord Rezzer.

Feeling helpless to resist the Hive's commands, the constant buzzing in my head that never completely went away, that just made me edgier. The battle against the internal enemy was constant. This Prillon before me was the latest outlet available, and I planned to make him miserable. Beat him bloody. Let the beast have some fun. Give him what he wanted.

I saw the hopeless rage in the Prillon warrior's golden eyes. He was new here. I didn't know his name, but I didn't need to. I recognized the wrath, the trapped feeling. We all did. Every single warrior banished was here on The Colony, not by choice, but because we'd been *contaminated* with Hive technology. Captured. Tortured. *Modified.*

We were no longer wanted by the people on our home planets, the people we'd sacrificed for. We were too dangerous.

Me, especially.

I wanted to hate the policy that required all contaminated warriors to live out the rest of their lives here, either working in the mines or protecting those who did, but I couldn't. The truth was that we *were* dangerous. Unstable. The Hive implants had strange effects on some warriors. And some, like me, never quite got them out of our heads. For me, the constant hum never left. Not even here, where the planet's defense systems were designed to keep out Hive communication frequencies.

But then, from what I'd been told, the Hive were here, hiding in the caves below the surface. Someday, there would be a reckoning, and then I'd hunt them, kill them. Tearing drones in half with my bare hands would bring me nothing but pleasure. Other than a mate's warm, wet pussy—which I had no hope of enjoying—killing the Hive was all I could think about.

Unfortunately, Governor Rone, the hard-ass Prillon warrior who ran Base 3, didn't feel turning me loose in the caves was a good idea. Not even during simple training runs for a new batch of Coalition Academy cadets. The training program was experimental, the caves below the surface a perfect simulation of several planets that were battle zones, hotbeds of Hive activity.

The Governor was right. First sight of a Hive here on The Colony, or of their leader, the Prillon warrior, Krael —the fucking traitor—and the beast would own me. There would be no coming back, no control.

By the gods, I wouldn't even try. I'd eviscerate them with my bare hands and howl with joy while doing it.

Fueled by my thoughts and the coming fight, the beast rose within me, eager and strong. I pushed back. Fought for control. Focused on the threat before me. His face. His fists. The lightness of his steps in the soft dirt. He was not a young, inexperienced fighter. He was a Prillon warrior in his prime. Strong. Fast. Deadly. And he'd just arrived after his own personal hell with the Hive.

Not that it would save him from a solid beating, but it would at least make the fight interesting.

We paced. Ready.

I heard her again. My cock, already hard, throbbed painfully.

The beast clawed at my insides, fighting to break free. Not to fight the Prillon. For her.

It wanted *her*.

Fuck.

Gods help me if she was the mate of a Colony warrior, or some innocent young cadet barely more than a child.

Keeping the Prillon on the edge of my vision, I scanned the crowd again. Found her.

Stilled. Stopped breathing.

By the gods, she was beautiful. Golden hair was pulled back from her face, and my first instinct was to break it free from whatever held it. Her eyes were like glaciers, too blue to be real. And she was human. I recognized her species from meeting Governor Rone's mate, Rachel, and because the warrior who had saved my life before coming here, one of the bravest fighters I'd ever met, was a female from Earth. A female who had earned my loyalty and respect. Commander Chloe Phan.

But her eyes had been dark. Her hair black. And she'd been small and mated to a Prillon warrior and a human I respected, the human who'd saved my life, Captain Seth Mills. I'd known the fearless commander wasn't mine. But the knowing had been easy. My beast hadn't been interested in her as a potential mate.

This human was completely different.

Fascinating.

Every curve was outlined to perfection by a tight black uniform, and I recognized the design as belonging to one of the instructors from the Coalition Academy on Zioria. Her hair was golden, her eyes a liquid blue that made me feel like I was falling. Her lips were a pale pink, and she was tall. Curvy. Her breasts were large and would be paradise in my hands. My mouth. I wondered what she tasted like. Her skin. Her kiss. Her hot, wet pussy juices flowing over my tongue as I made her scream.

She was not a child but a woman who knew what she wanted.

Our gazes met. Held. Locked.

The Prillon warrior paced. I ignored him. He was irrelevant now. My beast had other priorities. If my opponent wanted to bleed, he'd have to find another to entertain him.

I wanted the female. And from the way her gaze lingered on me, held mine, I knew she wouldn't resist.

She was mine.

The Prillon charged but I was no longer in the mood to fight. I wanted to fuck. Taste.

Claim.

I had planned to toy with the warrior, let him hit me a few times, draw some blood, let him bleed off some of his angst and wear himself out before I ended him. But I no longer felt accommodating.

Allowing the beast to surge for a moment, I swung hard, taking the glancing punch the Prillon landed on my chest. I connected with his jaw, felt the bone crack, knew they would rush a ReGen wand into the pit to stabilize him before shutting him down in a ReGen pod for a few hours to make sure I hadn't damaged his brain.

He hit the ground, unconscious, and I glanced at the medical crew to make sure they were coming. They had been waiting, ready. They'd seen it all before, knowing how this would end, but expecting me to play with my prey before I took him down.

The crowd was divided, half of the warriors cheering, a fair number booing the lack of a show. They were irrelevant. I only cared about one of them. Lifting my gaze, I found her in the crowd once more.

She had another female with her, and from the looks of things, they were talking about me.

Good.

I didn't want her thinking about anyone else. *Seeing* anyone else.

The Prillon rolled on the ground, groaning as they worked on his jaw. I walked past him toward the female.

He was no longer a concern. He was out of my way. And what I wanted was right in front of me.

I got closer, my beast cooperating, for once in perfect accord with what I wanted. We both wanted her. Hot. Naked. Open. Taking what we wanted to give her. Fucking hard and fast. Slow. Making her lose control. Making her give us everything.

I reached the edge of the arena and looked up to where she sat in the stands. Her blue eyes remained glued to me and I crooked my finger at her. She knew. She knew what I wanted. *Her.* We both knew how this was going to go. I could see an equal lust in her blue eyes.

She glanced at her friend, her delicate skin turning an intriguing shade of pink. She bit her lip as she turned back to me. I held out my hand and waited. Patient. She would come to me. The pull between us was elemental. Too strong for her to resist. My cock was so hard it was a constant ache. For her. Only for her.

Thank the gods she didn't make me wait long. The crowd was hushed, the other warriors and cadets watching with fascination as she walked down the steps and stopped before me, close enough to touch.

Gently, slowly, with a reverence I had no idea I could feel, I reached up and traced the softness of her cheek with my fingers.

The first contact jolted me, the rush better than any fight, any victory. The beast was frenzied, pushing at my skin, my mind, demanding to taste her. Touch her. Fill her with his seed. My thoughts went to the mating cuffs in my rooms and I knew what he wanted. What we both wanted. The miracle I had just found.

My mate.

"Mine." The word burst from me, beast and man both making sure every warrior heard my vow. *Mine.* I had staked my claim. If anyone touched her, hurt her, tried to take her from me, I would destroy them. Harder and more ruthlessly than I had with the Prillon in the middle of the pit.

Reaching over the barrier, I lifted her. She cooperated, swinging her legs over the waist high wall. When she would have put her feet on the ground, I swooped her up and carried her cradled against my chest.

Mine. Mine. Mine.

The thought consumed me until I couldn't talk. Couldn't think. Gods help me, if she resisted, I wasn't sure I could control the beast inside me. He was gone, so far gone. I knew if she denied me, walking away from her would be the last thing I remembered.

She *should* refuse me. I wasn't worthy of being a mate, but my beast disagreed, especially now with *her* in my hold. I would do it, let her go. For her. And then the others would have to put me down. Execute me. End my fucking misery, because now that I held her, I knew I could never walk away from her. Not and stay sane.

The beast was tired of waiting, and I was tired of fighting him.

Stretching my legs, I quickened my steps. The corridors were empty, everyone either in the fighting pits ready for the next face-off or in the new garden where most of us took our meals so we could watch the mated couples' children and feel normal again. Like maybe we weren't monsters.

"Where are you taking me?" Her soft question calmed some of the madness and I cleared my throat so I could answer her. I didn't want to scare her. She hadn't changed her mind. In fact, she was resting in my arms, her cheek pressed to my chest, her arms around my neck like she belonged there.

She did.

"To my room."

Her soft laugh was sexy as hell and my cock pulsed like an ion blaster. There was no question she could feel the hard length against the side of her hip. Good. She knew what was coming, how she affected me. I wondered if I affected her in the same way, if her nipples were hard points, her pussy a sticky, hot mess.

"Is it far, your room?" she asked breathlessly. "Because you are sex on a stick and I really don't want to wait." Her nails clawed into my shoulders.

Sex on a stick? I had no idea what the strange Earth term meant, even with the NPU, but it sounded like it was in my favor. As to the rest of what she'd said...

The beast roared and I had no hope of holding him back.

She wanted me.

Now.

My rooms were too far.

Yes. Too Far.

The next thing I knew I had her standing before me, pressed against the wall, her wrists held over her head with my left hand as I cradled her ass with my right. The soft feel of it in my palm made me groan. The beast took over, my muscles grew, my body exploded into *more*. Bigger. Stronger. Faster. I pressed the heat of her core to my hard cock. There could be no mistake. No question about what I wanted. What I needed.

Now.

Hungry. Gods, I was hungry. For her.

Her eyes were huge as she looked me over. Watched as I changed because of her. The extra foot of height. The enlarged jaw. Shoulders more than double the width of hers. We were both breathing hard, our lips so close I could taste her sweet breath on my tongue. The scent of her skin invaded my lungs and I knew I would never get her out of my system, never forget this moment.

"What's your name?" she asked, her head angled up so she could look at me. In beast mode, she was so much smaller.

"Angh," I said, lifting her up with the one hand on her ass, my one leg inserted between hers so we were almost eye level. I felt the heat of her pussy on my thigh.

"I'm Kira."

Her name was simple. Straightforward. Feminine. It suited. *Kira.* My mate's name was Kira. I blinked, holding her gaze, waiting for her to adjust to the presence of not the Atlan warrior, but my beast. For her eyes to shift from hungry and eager to fearful. Repulsed. I waited for her to push against me, to force me to put her down so she could run, scream. I anticipated the one word that would condemn me—*no.*

And yet, as the seconds ticked by, I didn't see any of that. She was panting. Her eyes became darker, like the wildest of storms over my home planet. Her cheeks flushed a glorious pink—the color I imagined her pussy to be. I took in every detail. Growled when her tongue flicked out and she licked her full lips.

"So, this is beast mode?"

Her gaze roamed over me with blatant appreciation,

lingered on my bare chest. My neck. My lips. "I've heard about it. Read about it. God. It's—you're—wow." She smiled, her first smile, and everything within me stilled. My balls ached, my cock dripped the pre-cum that could no longer be contained. I was hers. Just like that, she owned me.

"Want you."

Two words. It was all I could manage, and on a growl. My room was on the other side of the base, two floors and a half mile of long hallways away. It might as well have been on another planet. I'd never make it. Not now. Impossible. I wasn't sure if it was even possible to walk with my cock this hard, the way it continued to thicken and swell down my inner thigh.

"Here?"

"Now." I shifted my leg, pressed my thigh against where I knew her clit was hidden by her uniform. She gasped, her head tilted back against the wall as she moved in sync with me, her hips gyrating and humping my leg, taking her pleasure as she wanted.

I'd never seen anything more beautiful.

"Okay. Now. God, you're hot. So hot. Yes. I want you." She lifted her legs, wrapped them around my hips, then froze. I held still, a predator, waiting, my cock now perfectly aligned to slip into her pussy, if only our clothes weren't in the way. Her whispered confession was ragged, as if she was having trouble breathing. "I don't normally do this. God, I don't know what the hell is happening to me. I—"

I cut her off with a kiss.

Our first kiss.

Our *last* first kiss.

The taste of her consumed me. I devoured her, my tongue driving deeply to savor her sweetness, to swallow her moan of satisfaction. She was exquisite. Unique. Submissive. I demanded and she gave. I hungered and she let me drown in her, melting into my arms. She kissed me back, keeping nothing of herself. She demanded as much as she gave, hungered like I did.

It was heaven. A heaven I thought I'd never sample.

Her nipples were hard peaks beneath her uniform. The wet heat of her drifted up to me, the beast scented her arousal and I released the clasp on the side of her pants, pulled them down to the tops of her thighs after she loosened her legs' tight hold about my waist to help me do so, just enough to give me the access I wanted.

Needed.

"Oh my god, yes." She curved her body, bringing her knees up toward her chest to give me access to her core. Her pants were bunched and stretched tightly across her thighs, but her pussy was right there. Open. The punch of her scent hit me with more strength than anything I'd ever felt in the pit.

I slipped a finger through her soft folds. Pushed inside.

She was perfect. Hot. Dripping wet. Ready. She gasped at the intrusion, writhed, clenched her inner walls as if to pull me in deeper. As if she wanted more.

"Kira." The beast growled her name as I held her wrists and freed my cock, my fingers slick with her desire.

"Angh." She arched her back, pushing toward me, demanding I fill her. Fuck her.

I'd never seen anything like her. Had no idea a female so desirable existed. I could deny her nothing.

Lining up my cock, I pressed forward gently. I was so

much bigger than she was. In beast mode, my cock was going to stretch her wide, fill her deep. I didn't want to hurt her.

Her pussy clamped down on the head of my cock like a fist and she thrashed, tugging at my hold on her wrists. I froze, afraid I was hurting her. I'd rather die than hurt her.

Her eyes opened, met mine. "So good. Don't stop. Please, don't stop."

Trembling now, I pushed my hips forward, stretching her. Filling her. She was so hot. So tight. So wet. Her inner walls rippled in response to being opened so wide, adjusted to a beast's cock. The beast shuddered at the feel, calm. Content to focus on our mate. To fuck her. Fill her with our seed. Mark her. Claim her. "Mine."

"Angh." Her head was back, her eyes closed. Her lips glistened from my kiss.

I needed more.

Bending low, I kissed her again as I drove my cock deep and stayed there, up against her womb where I would plant my seed and my claim. I held her there with a hand at the base of her spine, supported her weight so she didn't have to. I didn't want her to do anything but *feel*. I lifted her onto my cock, grinding her small body against me as I fucked her with both cock and tongue. I was inside her. Fucking her. Tasting her. The wet sounds of our joining filled the hallway, our ragged pants the only other sound.

Mine.

I pulled back, thrust deep. I swallowed her scream as her pussy pulsed around me, her body giving me what I demanded. Surrender.

She came within a minute, bucking and arching in my arms like a wild thing. She didn't hold back. Didn't hide her pleasure. The sight of her was incredible, the look of bliss, of pure pleasure on her face made my beast preen, my cock pulse, my balls draw up. And knowing I'd brought her to the edge and over, that she was mine, pushed me to the razor's edge.

The tight fist of her pussy on my cock forced me over and I lifted my head with a roar as my seed pumped into her. Half the base heard me, but I didn't give a shit. She was mine, and I was proud for everyone to know my mate was so perfect she gave me the most exquisite of pleasure.

For long seconds I held her, my cock buried deep, still hard. Seed still spurting from me. It was as if I'd stored it all up, saving it all for her, for her womb.

I expected the beast to fade, but he remained. Demanding. Needy. He wasn't done. A quick fuck wasn't all the beast needed. He wanted our mating cuffs on her wrists. On ours.

I lowered my forehead to hers and fought for words.

"More."

She laughed, the sound filled with happiness. Nodded. "Does it have to be in the hallway?"

I growled and pulled out of her wet heat, my cock not at all happy about it as I lowered her to her feet, tucked it back into my pants. I stepped back just enough so she could straighten her clothing and my beast didn't like seeing her covered up again. But knowing my seed was deep inside her, slipping out of her as our scents mingled was enough. For now.

"Naked."

Fuck. She was really going to think I was a crude

animal. But the beast was in control now, and he was raw. There would be no controlling him until I was hers. Completely. Officially. I needed the mating cuffs on my wrists, needed the visual reminder that I belonged to her now. Needed the stinging pain of separation they caused to help me control the beast. We both needed the reminder that I had someone to protect, to love, to serve. Beast and man both needed a reason to keep on fighting.

Kira held out her hand to me, exactly as I had done to her outside, in the arena. She was ruffled now, looked well fucked. A sweaty brow, her pale hair was damp from our exertions, her cheeks flushed, her lips red and swollen, all blatant signs of my claim.

I didn't take her hand. Instead, I lifted her into my arms once again and carried her away.

3

$\mathcal{K}$ira, *The Colony, Angh's quarters*

"You're awake," Angh said, his sleepy voice a rough murmur close to my ear. We were spooned in his big bed, my head resting on his thick biceps, his other arm over my waist and cupping my bare breast. I felt every hard inch of him against my back, even his legs, as they were bent and nestled to the full length of mine.

I smiled into the dark room. "So are you." I wiggled my hips against the thick hardness growing, thickening, prodding at my back.

He grunted, shifting, and pressed his hips forward so his cock slid along the seam of my bottom, between my legs, spreading my swollen pussy lips open from behind as he coated himself in the instant flood of welcoming heat. Just that fast, I was wet. Hot. Ready.

"Again?" I asked, licking my lips. My pussy was a little

sore. How could it not be? An Atlan's cock was huge—bigger than any images of a porn star I'd ever seen on Earth—and that wasn't even in beast mode. Then...*god.* Just the memory brought me closer to orgasm.

That was why, when he'd carried me back to his room, he'd taken me to his shower—an oversized one, I assumed to accommodate his beast—and cleaned every inch of me, then dropped to his knees and made me come with his mouth. To say Angh wielded his tongue with as much precision as his huge cock was an understatement.

And to say he was voracious? The three orgasms he gave me beneath the hot spray before my legs gave out was proof of that.

"My cock will never go down. Not with you nearby, with the taste of you on my tongue, the hot feel of your pussy all over my cock, your scent in my lungs."

He was quite the caveman, and I loved it. This wasn't just a wild night of fucking. The connection was something I couldn't describe. Lying here, snoozing in his embrace felt comfortable, right. Perfect. It wasn't awkward. I wasn't worried that I'd made a stupid mistake or wondering how I could slip out without waking him. There would be no walk of shame. I didn't regret a single moment of the time we'd spent together. And I loved knowing I aroused him, that his cock wouldn't go down with me nearby.

It was heady and made me feel powerful. Me, all five feet plus of me, could bring an Atlan beast to his knees. I had done just that, in the shower.

I giggled. Until he lifted my leg up over his thigh and slid into me from behind.

"Angh..." I turned my head into his bicep, bit gently as

he filled me, stretched me. His scent surrounded me and I was so tender, so sensitive, that when his hand moved from my nipple, roamed over my stomach and down to my clit, my pussy was in spasm, my orgasm rolling through me before he had completed the journey.

He stroked me twice. Three times. Until I was shaking and boneless, content to let him have his way with me. Again.

Angh shifted, pulling out despite my moan of protest. He rolled me so I was on my back and he was up on his elbow, looking down at me. "Lights, ten percent," he said aloud, the room's comm unit responding by adding a hint of brightness to the wall sconces.

His dark eyes met mine. Held. I'd never had a man look at me with such intensity, such focus and need before. He *wanted* me.

This was crazy. Insane. I couldn't have him. Well, I could have him *now*. In his room, his bed—hell, his shower—but that was it. I could savor a huge cock while I was still here on The Colony. Get a stockpile of orgasms to hold me for a long time. When I'd told Melody I didn't want a mate, it was the truth. I hadn't been looking for one, hadn't even considered the possibility.

I was an instructor. I could be mated and keep that job. There was no issue at the Coalition Academy with that; if there was one, they wouldn't have many instructors. Vikens and especially Everians couldn't be apart from a mate. Prillons had the collars that kept them *connected*. No one wanted to deal with a pissed-off Prillon warrior. And an unmated Atlan beast with enough experience to keep the young, aggressive males in line? No freaking way.

But working for the I.C. was another matter. Having a

mate was dangerous. Not only could the enemy use the connection, the bond with another person, as a weakness, but the mortality rate was high. Hell, it was high for all fighters, but the missions I went on were dangerous. If we didn't succeed, we didn't come home. Behind enemy lines and usually classified, the missions we went on didn't even exist in any Coalition files. No records were kept. We were as *black* as black ops got.

My job didn't *exist.*

"You are beautiful, Kira," Angh said, his hand stroking over my hair, his thumb sliding along my cheek with each pass. "Beautiful and brave and perfect."

Wow. That was a lot. I frowned and he smoothed away the wrinkle. "So are you," I replied, stating the obvious. He was beautiful. All male perfection.

"No, mate. I *want* you. The real you. I need to know everything about you."

I licked my lips at that, having no idea how to reply. There was a lot I couldn't tell him. Like half of my life.

"My beast is pleased with you."

I smiled then, not used to being with a man who had an internal...animal that controlled him, at least in more *heated* moments. Seeing Angh now, the beast had receded and he was normal sized, in other words, huge. But he could say more than one word at a time. Could do more than grunt.

"I'm glad," I replied. "I'm pleased with your beast, too. Especially that thing he did—"

Angh silenced me with a kiss. Not a simple peck, but an all-out assault. I gasped and he took the opportunity for his tongue to find mine. He licked, stroked, ravaged. He didn't let up, didn't relent on his excellent kissing until my mind went hazy, my body went pliant and my pussy ached for his cock. *Again.* I couldn't get enough.

Only then did he lift his head. He leaned back, reached, but I couldn't see for what. His broad chest blocked everything. I shivered when he set four metal cuffs on my chest, right there in the dip between my breasts. They clanked as they bumped. I watched them rise and fall with my breathing, my nipples hardened with their coolness.

He lifted one, put it on his wrist. Like Wonder Woman bracelets, but silver-toned, they were several inches wide. Engraved into them was a pattern of swirls and designs that looked custom. Handmade.

"My beast sees your lush curves, wants you again."

"Have me," I begged.

His eyes darkened, his jaw clenched and his nostrils flared as he studied me. "You know how big I am, how tight the fit in your snug pussy. You didn't even take all of my beast cock."

That I hadn't known. I'd been too lost in my need and I *felt* full. How could there possibly be *more?*

"I will have you again, mate, but I must control my beast, or he will take you. Fill you again. You would not be able to walk tomorrow."

I thought of how I'd look hobbling to transport in a few hours. It would be the worst walk of shame imaginable, being bowlegged and sore from a wild night of fucking a beast cock. It was one thing to have all of the cadets know that I had a wild night with an Atlan—I was sure one or two of them had probably found an eager fighter for a night of fun themselves—but to wince when I walked would be too much. I'd never live it down, not as the instructor for the mission. There were lines the instructors, serving as role models and leaders, were not allowed to cross, and showing up bow-legged and sore was definitely way over that line.

"The cuffs will control your beast?" I asked. I knew of them, had seen them on the Atlan instructors at the Academy, but I didn't spend time in their area. The beasts pretty much kept to themselves. They voted for their own commanders and formed their own fighting units. We shared space at the training grounds on Zioria, but that was all. And I did not go on missions for the I.C. with any Atlans. They were widely considered to be too unstable, too unpredictable. Wild.

Surprise, surprise, I really *liked* wild.

"They do. I hope the nap was enough, for I will now be able to fuck you all night. Be prepared, female, to be filled with my cock until dawn."

My eyes flared at his dirty words, but I realized they weren't just talk, they were a promise. With ease, he shifted me to my side once again and settled back behind me. The three remaining cuffs slid to the bed in front of me.

He bent my knees and pushed my thighs up toward my chest, my pussy wet and on display. Angh settled his hips between my thighs and opened me up, the head of his cock brushing over my slick folds, settling at my entrance.

I gasped at the feel of him as he pressed in, just so the broad crown breached me, settled just inside. I clenched about him, trying to pull him deeper, but he held himself still. Grabbing the large cuff, he wrapped it about his other wrist, clicked it in place. He nudged in a touch further and my back came up off the bed, the smaller cuffs falling onto the warm sheets next to me. Forgotten.

"Angh," I gasped, shifting and trying to take more of him.

"Your cuffs, Kira, are there, waiting for you."

"Mine?" I asked, breathless. My thoughts were on the tip of his cock and nothing else. I had no idea there were so many delicious nerve endings just inside of me, that having a big—no, huge—cock in me made them all come to life. I wanted more. Needed it.

"I cannot put them on your wrists. You must lock them in place. My beast desires to see them on your body, but you must consent, must choose willingly. Blatantly and without coercion."

I pushed the two cuffs out of the way and wiggled away from him. He let me go—no way would I be able to move if he wanted me to remain—and I got up onto my knees so I looked down at him.

"Coercion? Coercion is sticking your hard cock in my pussy and denying me all of you, refusing to go deeper. I need you to fuck me." Gripping his shoulders, I directed him where I wanted him, on his back. Thank God he let me have my way, because he was a giant and there was no way I could force him to move a single hair on his head unless he wanted to move it. Apparently, he was content to let me have my way. For now.

In fact, his eyes widened and he grinned.

"You are feisty," he said, settling onto his back and putting an arm behind his head. He looked so casual, so relaxed, even with his cock jutting toward the ceiling, the broad head of it glistening from being inside me. His gaze roved over me, slow and full of appreciation, stopping at my breasts and then stalling entirely at the juncture of my thighs. It seemed his beast was soothed because he wasn't jumping me. Like this, Angh was completely different. Calm, perhaps even a touch playful.

I smiled. "I am an Academy instructor, which means I do like to be in charge."

He huffed out a small laugh, reached up and stroked his knuckles over my nipple, watched it as it went hard. "You want to be in charge of your beast?" he asked.

Yeah, he was definitely playful. It was my turn to look my fill. From the dark hair that was loose and wild on his head to his wicked smile, broad shoulders, smattering of dark hair on his chest that tapered to his navel. And there, his abs, rippled and spectacular. And speaking of spectacular, the massive cock between his legs, the large, virile balls beneath. It was hard not to stop there, but his thighs were massive, bigger perhaps than my waist. Well-muscled, solid. Sturdy. Even his feet were hot and I had no trace of a foot fetish.

"Yes, I do," I said, licking my lips. "I want you." The question was, where to start?

"Very well. Do as you wish."

I flicked my gaze up to his, saw that he was serious. *Oh, this was going to be fun.* Could Angh and his beast remain still as I had my way with him? Teased him? Sucked him off? Played and tasted and rode him like I wanted to? He was bigger, heavier and could dominate me if he wished—and he had earlier. But now, he intended to remain still and let me take control.

I felt wicked and powerful as I wondered how long he would hold out. I intended to find out. Leaning forward, I gave him a quick, gentle kiss. Keeping my eyes open as I did so, we watched each other and I savored the less frantic look on his face. The Atlan was in charge now, Angh, and I liked him. So much.

"You'll stay still?"

"Yes."

"No matter what?" I countered.

"No matter what."

I shifted on my knees, moved closer to his hips. "We'll see about that," I said, just before I lowered my head and took his cock into my mouth.

He jolted as if electrocuted. I gasped, realizing there was absolutely no way I could take all of him in my mouth. If it wasn't going to all cram into my pussy, it wasn't fitting my throat. I had a gag reflex and I'd never deep throated anyone before. So I put my hands on the base of his cock, stacking them one on top of the other and worked him with fists and mouth at the same time.

He was warm and his skin was so smooth, but the hard feel of his need beneath, the way he swelled and grew as I licked and sucked was heady, and no pun intended. Pre-cum coated my tongue as he tensed and growled, bucked and did everything he could not to touch me. I reveled in his flavor, the tangy essence of him.

"Mate, you are going to be the death of me, and I am going to enjoy it immensely."

Hollowing my cheeks, I gave him one last suck before lifting my head, licking my lips.

"Are you wet and ready for my cock?" he asked.

I shifted back up toward his head, studied him. This had been a wild night so far. I'd pushed my inhibitions to the side and it had been reckless and wonderful. I had no reason to stop now. Putting my hands on his chest, I carefully tossed a leg over so I straddled his upper torso. We'd bathed, and I felt bold. Wild. I'd never *asked* a man to feast on my pussy, but he wasn't a man. He was an Atlan. A beast. He seemed more primal, somehow. Primitive and rough and my inhibitions were nowhere to be found. I wanted him sucking on me. Fucking me with his mouth and fingers and tongue. I wanted to kiss him and taste my need on his lips.

He frowned, looking up at me. His hands were still behind his head, but I could see the silver of his cuffs and was grateful that they helped him control himself so that I could have this moment.

Sweat dotted his brow and his jaw was tense. Dark eyes filled with lust. Nostrils flared. His chest was heaving beneath me and I would have sworn his hands were trembling. He was holding back, just for me, and the knowledge made me feel powerful and wicked. So hot. Wet and ready? That felt like a week ago. Now I was desperate.

"I don't know," I said, answering his question. "Why don't you find out for me?"

I slid off his torso so I was straddling his face, hovering directly above him, my pussy inches from his lips and my knees landing where his arms had been, forcing him to move them out of my way. I was on a mission.

His hands came around, cupped my bottom as he groaned. "Mate, right here. This is where I want to die."

I didn't have any time to think, for he pulled me down and ate me. There was no other word for it. His mouth was voracious, his tongue skilled. I planted my hands on the wall, for there was nothing else I could do.

"So much for being in control," I murmured, just before I cried out his name.

His response to taking over was a flat-tongued lick and a deep, beast growl of pleasure. He worked me until I came, his tongue thrusting deeply as my pussy went into uncontrollable spasms.

When I could move, I moved down his body and grabbed his hard length, placed him where I needed him, and took him deep as he arched up off the bed. I slid up and down, my hand so small on his chest it was comical to think I could hold him down. But I did. He stayed still, as he'd promised, and let me take my fill.

"Don't move, Warlord. You're mine right now."

"I am yours." He thrust upward, his hips rising to meet me and I gasped at the extra pressure on my womb, the way his body bumped my clit. I rode him until I came again and collapsed against his chest, his cock still buried deep.

"I can't take anymore. It's too much."

Angh just laughed and rolled both of us over, his cock stroking in and out of my body with a slow, lazy rhythm that had me moaning and clutching at his shoulders. His hair. I wrapped my legs around his hips and tilted my body to take him deeper. Begged him to go faster.

He refused, building me into a frantic mess, never adjusting his pace, holding my hips trapped to the bed when I tried to force the pace.

His dominance was my undoing, the unyielding hold of his hands on my hips as he fucked me drove me out of my mind. My body exploded. My brain turned to mush. There was no more Kira, there was only him.

He fucked me as I came, his cock stroking over my

pulsing core. Dragging out the orgasm, stretching my inner muscles, moving inside me. Relentless. Disciplined. Controlled.

My body was shaking, a hot mess. I couldn't breathe. I couldn't think. I could only feel the hard slide of him filling me up over and over. Stretching me wide. Making me his. And the fire built again. He knew when I gave in, when I let the rush wash over me and the orgasm started to build. And build.

"Angh!" I was begging. I wasn't sure if I wanted him to go fast or slow. Hard or gentle. I didn't know what I needed. I just...*needed.*

His lips settled over my ear, his voice a deep rumble that made my pussy clench down on his cock like a fist. "You're mine, Kira. Mine."

The simple declaration pushed me over the edge and he hovered, watching me like I was the only thing in the universe that existed. When I opened my eyes, our gazes locked and the heat, the *possession* I saw in his eyes, made me feel more vulnerable than I'd ever felt in my life. And still, he moved. Filled me. Made me whimper and say his name. Over and over.

It was going to be a long night.

I just had to make sure I was on that transport pad at dawn. I had to go back to the Coalition Academy on time. If I missed my transport window, it would be at least two days before I could get approval for another of that distance, and I had a mission briefing thirty minutes after our scheduled return. I had to go. Someone's life depended on it. And a two-day delay *would* be the ultimate walk of shame. *Sorry, Vice Admiral, I couldn't go on the mission because I was too busy fucking a beast.*

Not happening. But based on the way Angh possessed my pussy, I doubted he would let me out of his bed any time soon. It would be time to leave soon enough, but not yet. Not now. Now was for me. And him. For *this*.

I pulled his head down, way down, for a kiss and let him fuck me. Fill me. Let myself feel like I wasn't alone in the big, bad universe. Like someone cared.

No, I was not in a hurry to leave him. Not yet. I stopped worrying about tomorrow and gave myself over to the Atlan and his beast.

Morning was so, so far away.

4

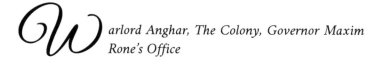

arlord Anghar, The Colony, Governor Maxim Rone's Office

"DEMAND THEY RETURN AT ONCE," I SNAPPED, MY VOICE like the boom of a cannon.

I paced the Governor's office, a tough Prillon bastard named Ryston stood just inside the door. He'd been altered to become a Hive Scout. His vision and senses enhanced. His temple shimmered silver. His implants were visible, unlike the Prillon Tyran, who stood outside.

Tyran had microscopic Hive enhancements woven through every major muscle group in his body. The implants made him nearly as strong as a beast in full frenzy.

Tyran was mated to Kristen. Ryston, however, was the governor's second, and together, they were mated to Rachel, who Ryston had forced to sit due to her advanced pregnancy.

The copper colored collars around all three of their necks made my beast furious. It was a sign of their connection, their fucking bond that was only shared by mates. I felt the weight of the cuffs on my wrists, but they meant nothing since their match was attached to my belt, and not on Kira.

Thank the gods, the cuffs, and the scent of her on my skin, were holding the beast at bay. For now. The stinging pain from the cuffs a constant reminder that she was mine.

Kira was mine. My mate. My beast knew the truth and so did I. I had no idea why she had left me while I slept, but I would find out. Demand answers. And then fuck her until she knew exactly who she belonged to and never doubted again.

Maxim was in my fucking way. *His* mate was safe and happy, sitting beside him with his collar around her neck and his child growing large in her womb. Judging by the sympathy directed at me in Rachel's dark eyes, this conversation was going nowhere good.

Besides the three of them in the room, there was also the silver-eyed human, Lieutenant Washington. Denzel. He was dark skinned, like a Prillon warrior, but his eyes were unnerving. Solid metallic and shiny. And he had the strength of a warrior five times his size thanks to the rest of the Hive implants in his body. I ignored him and he remained quiet and watchful.

"The transport window to Zioria is closed for another thirty-six hours. We've been over this, Angh," the governor reminded me. "I realize you want to go after your mate, but I can't move planets for you."

"Tell that to my beast." The beast was raging. I was

holding on by a thread, and the copper skinned Prillon knew it.

So did his mate.

Rachel stood, albeit clumsily with her huge belly, and walked toward me. She was lovely, smaller than my Kira, with dark brown hair and warm brown eyes. Behind me, the golden Prillon, Ryston, bristled, but she held up her hand and waved him down. I would never hurt her. Not if I was in control. But if he touched me, or tried to take me down, that control might just snap. Maybe that was why Denzel and Tyran were all here, making four warriors who might try to control me if need be.

My beast all but laughed. *As if.*

The tiny hand she placed on my forearm was meant to soothe, but her touch irritated instead. She wasn't mine. Wasn't Kira.

"I'm sorry, Angh. She probably didn't know what the cuffs meant. They don't exactly explain anything to us Earth girls before we're processed and transported to our mates."

"She's not an Interstellar Bride, Lady Rone," I clarified. "She's an instructor at the Coalition Academy. I need to go after her. I need answers."

Kira's much smaller mating cuffs hung from a small hook attached to my armor. I couldn't bear to look at them, her rejection hurt too much. The fact that she'd left me, sneaked out of my bed in the darkest hours before dawn and left the fucking planet was proof of that rejection. Proof also of how replete and sated I had been, how relaxed my beast had been in her presence, to sleep through her departure. I barely slept, ever, because of the buzzing in my skull, but the one fucking time I had, she'd slipped away.

Yes, the transport for the group from the Academy had been scheduled and she was the group's leader, but she didn't *have* to escort them. They weren't children she was shepherding back to a kinder program. These were adults from all over the galaxy who didn't need *my* mate to fucking hold their hands.

What was a job when it came to mates? I'd heard of Everians abandoning everything when their mark awakened. Hell, I'd finished the Prillon in the pit with one punch solely because I *saw* Kira, knew she'd be mine and couldn't wait another second to have her.

If she'd wanted me, she'd have stayed. If she'd wanted me, she'd have put on the mating cuffs. Was Rachel right? Had she really not known what they meant? What sneaking out would do to me? Had an Earth woman, one intelligent and brave enough to have the prestigious job of Academy instructor, not *known*?

Yet somehow, I clung to hope, to Lady Rone's words like they were a lifeline, because the alternative was too terrible to endure.

My mate didn't want me. She'd just wanted my cock.

I'd pleasured her well. Fucked her quick and hard in a damned hallway; how had she not known from that exactly how desperate I was for her? After that, when my beast had been initially sated, I'd feasted on her pussy. Made her scream and beg and milk my cock all night. She'd been well satisfied. Well-fucked. Filled with seed.

Claimed.

I'd vowed to be hers, said the words and placed the mating cuffs on my wrists to prove it. I had bathed and fed her, cared for her in every way I could in such a short time. I had done everything to ensure her pleasure, to impress her. I'd shown her my beast and bested the Prillon in the pit. I should have been worthy.

It seemed, I wasn't.

I was contaminated. Perhaps I had been correct all along. The Colony was no place for worthy females. What if she had been processed as an Interstellar Bride and matched to someone else? A truly worthy warrior. Someone who was whole and could offer her a better life, one not on the distant and barren Colony.

Perhaps that was the reason she had not placed them on her wrists. Had she known she was matched to another?

The thought made my beast rage and I stepped back, away from Rachel, her innocent touch a trigger I did not need, not when my mate was gone and because of it, the Mating Fever was now upon me.

With a sigh, Rachel stepped back and Ryston walked to her quickly, pulling her away from me, behind me. I knew he wrapped her in his arms where they both watched as I confronted the Governor with my plans.

I focused my attention on the only person who could approve my trip. The only one who kept me from my mate. I narrowed my eyes, bit out the words, "I'm going after her."

"You're in Mating Fever." The cold, calculating accusation came from behind me, not from Ryston, but from the human, Denzel. I turned my head slowly, his cold, silver eyes unnerving no matter how many times I'd seen him. They reminded me of the Hive Integration Unit who had tortured me, altered my body, put this thing inside my head that buzzed, even now. I was never without the reminder that they had broken me.

There was no sympathy in Denzel's tone, and no room for lies.

"Yes." I nodded, although they didn't need my agreement to know the truth. "I was holding the fever at bay before. But having her here triggered it."

He nodded and looked at the governor. "I'll go with him to the Academy on Zioria. Help him find her."

"And what if she doesn't want to come back with you?" the governor asked.

I growled, the deep rumble filling the silence. "Then I don't come back." I shrugged, the answer no longer painful. I was ready to die. I'd been ready for a long time. Captain Mills, a fellow fighter and a ReCon team leader I'd worked with pre-Hive integration, had saved me even when I'd begged for him to finish me. I'd been ruined then and I was ruined now. There was no room left for fear, not for myself. But for Kira?

She could be in trouble right now. Hurting. Injured. She might need me, and I was here, half a galaxy away. She was out of my reach, and just the *possibility* of something being wrong made the beast insane with the need to see her, smell her, touch her, taste her, make sure she was safe and whole and well.

"No! Angh, that's...just no!" Rachel's voice was full of worry I didn't need. "There has to be another way!" Her protest was well-intentioned, but I was in full blown Mating Fever and the males in the room knew what that meant. If I didn't reunite with my mate soon, if she didn't accept my claim, voluntarily put the cuffs on her wrists and allow me to claim her in the official, Atlan way, I'd be a monster in truth. A cyborg enhanced beast who'd lost his mind. A killing machine unlike any other.

The cuffs I wore kept me sane. For now. But they wouldn't control the raging within me for long. I needed my mate nearby to soothe him, to keep him content. I would will the beast back, control myself until I knew the truth of her feelings.

The governor looked at Denzel. "If you go with him, it will fall to you." *To finish Warlord Anghar if need be.* He didn't say the last, but we all knew it.

I turned to assess the fighter's capabilities, both mentally and physically.

Our gazes locked. Held. The cold-blooded killer staring back at me would give no quarter if that's what was needed. "You have to tell her the truth," he said.

I shook my head. "No. I will not force her hand. She must make the choice to be my mate for herself."

"You're willing to die for your honor?" he asked.

I held his gaze so he'd understand. "No, I will die for her, for her happiness. I will not use coercion or manipulate her against her will. I will not accept a mate who chooses me out of pity. I would rather die." I paused, then clarified. "I *will* die first."

Denzel dropped his chin in a slight bow of respect. "So be it. I'll go with you. See it through."

Relieved, I tilted my head as well, in thanks. "Take an ion rifle. A blaster will just make me angry."

"I'll bring two." The human's silver gaze was steady. Solid.

Yes. He would do.

I turned back to Maxim and raised a brow. Clenched my fists. "I'm going after my mate. The lieutenant can accompany me. If she refuses my claim, he'll do what needs to be done."

The governor studied us both for a minute. The longest fucking minute of my life. "So be it. Those cuffs will only keep the fever in check for so long. Get your mate, or may the gods take you."

5

Kira, Sector 437, Battlegroup Karter, Shuttle Bay 9

"DAMN IT!" COMMANDER CHLOE PHAN PULLED HER helmet off and threw it against the side of the shuttle in a fit of anger. "This isn't working. That's the third time we've gone out there and we're no closer to taking that barrier down."

Chloe was a fellow Earth girl, fellow I.C. asset, and my exact opposite. She was beautiful and exotic, with straight ebony hair and dark green eyes. I was pale and colorless next to her with my blonde hair and milk-white skin. But she was human, smart as hell, and right now, she was giving voice to the rage I, too, felt. We'd been out on the edge of Sector 437 three times now, looking for the central command nodes of the newest weapon the Hive were using to control space, an invisible network of mines so powerful they could destroy an entire battlegroup in minutes.

And it had done just that less than two weeks ago.

Since these nodes were undetectable by the Coalition's current ship sensors, the Coalition had lost an entire battlegroup in a single day in Sector 19. Gone. Completely obliterated.

Because of this, Commander Grigg Zakar had shown up at I.C. Core Command—uninvited, which was borderline suicidal even for an angry Prillon—and demanded an I.C. asset with the brain implants be deployed to his battleship at once to keep the same thing from happening under his command.

The woman who'd gone with him, Erica James, was one of my best friends, a *make-love-not-war* hippie from Oregon. She was half black and half white...her mother was a hippie and her dad a rocket scientist. The woman was funny as hell, totally different and the most unexpected person I'd ever met on the front lines of our fight with the Hive.

No doubt, she was already rocking their world out there in Sector 17 with all those big, burly alpha-male aliens having to wait for her to hear things through the implant in the base of her skull. I'd spent more than a few hours with a grin on my face wondering how things were going and how the warriors out there were adapting to her obsession with 1970s-era Earth disco music. Thinking of a group of Atlan Warlords grooving to the Village People's song *Macho Man* almost made me burst out laughing.

Insane! But dancing or not dancing, Battlegroup Zakar was still fighting and still whole, so I figured she was doing her job. I hadn't heard of a group of Warlords and warriors going AWOL either.

Erica was doing her job, but Chloe and I were struggling. That brought my wandering attention back to the here and now. Sector 437, and the Battlegroup Karter. Especially since Chloe practically had smoke coming out of her ears. This battlegroup had its own problems. They weren't trapped, but they couldn't move freely either. I could transport in and out, go back to my day job at the Coalition Academy. Others could transport, too, and they could move supplies, but until we took down that damned barrier, the entire battlegroup wasn't moving anywhere. It was like being caught on a highway with a fifty-car pileup because of an invisible jackknifed eighteen-wheeler. No one was moving forward and because of the cars continuing to bunch up at the back, we were stuck.

In short, the Hive was winning, and none of us were happy about it.

"Then we'll go out again and again until we find what we're looking for, Commander." The Prillon who spoke to Chloe was a gorgeous specimen, an excellent pilot, and Chloe's mate. And while on the job, he called her by her title. I loved the way he respected her rank, her knowledge, even while being the blatant dominant. I didn't know much about her other mate, but knew he must have some serious balls because Chloe needed a strong-willed partner—*partners*—and a very gentle touch. Per the Prillon custom that they followed—I couldn't miss the matching collars about their necks—she had two mates, and she'd told me one was human, the other obviously very Prillon. How the hell *that* had happened, I had no idea. Two was one too many for me. One big Atlan was more than enough to satisfy my every need. I didn't know how I could survive two. I'd die from orgasm overdose. Inwardly, I shrugged, thinking it wasn't that bad of a way to go.

I thought of big, gorgeous, strong, sexy Angh. It still broke my heart, even with the depressing reminder of just how badly the war was going—and how much I was still needed—that I couldn't keep him. Leaving him asleep in his bed had been one of the hardest things I'd ever had to do.

"No, Dorian, we won't," Chloe argued back. "I can't do this alone. And *she—*" I was the *she* that Chloe pointed to with disgust— "can't hear them." The look she gave me was brutally honest and unapologetic. "Sorry, Kira, but your presence didn't help like we'd hoped."

"I can hear the Drones, but nothing else. I'm sorry." I sighed, knowing I hadn't been the least bit helpful on this mission. I'd been a failure, a dud and a complete waste of time. We'd discovered that when two of us with the implants were together, the sound was amplified. I was to be the *signal boost* for Chloe, but it hadn't worked. My implant hadn't done shit. *I'd* done shit for the mission.

"I know. I guess we should be counting our blessings that you heard the Hive trio that came for us on the surface of that asteroid. That saved our ass. I was too distracted looking for the mines."

I had saved us, but it was more luck than skill. We'd been ambushed, the Hive protecting their asset from the Coalition threat. Which meant we were getting close. But close didn't count for shit when an entire Battlegroup could go down in a matter of hours. I'd heard them coming and taken a hit near my elbow, blocking the Hive

Scout who'd tried to take me. But that was the last thing he'd ever done. I'd ended him with a blast from my ion rifle while Chloe and the Vice Admiral took care of his two friends.

And I'd been trying, *trying* to hear the larger Hive network chatter in my mind, as disturbing as that was. Every once in a while, I'd get a buzz in my head, but it always faded before I could grab onto it and go deeper, before I could make it easier for Chloe to hear. Like a breeze whispering to my mind and moving on.

"I'm trying. And they're right there. I can feel them, their energy, but it stays just out of reach." I didn't take her comments personally. It wasn't as if I had any control over the stupid implant. Or the Hive, for that matter. I was a tool, a piece of equipment, not a person when it came to this kind of mission.

"No one said you weren't, Captain." That was my commanding officer speaking, a Vice Admiral from Everis, one of the only women I'd ever met from that planet. She was also the only female Everian Hunter on the Coalition Fleet's asset list. Her name was Niobe, and she was the highest-ranking officer on Zioria, and in charge of the Coalition Academy, all the officers and cadets, and another of the I.C.'s hidden assets on the planet. We'd been on dozens of missions together, and although I didn't consider her a friend, I did respect her, and her judgment. "And you did save us today. Good job. We're getting close."

"We've *been* close for months." Chloe shrugged out of her space suit, her mate stepping forward to assist her, but she shrugged him off. "Thanks, Dorian. I got it. I just need a minute."

He nodded, stepped back. "Anything you need, mate. Ask and it is yours."

She smiled up at him and pressed her hand to his cheek, a wealth of intimate communication passing between the two that I envied. And missed. I had no doubt if he had the implant, the two of them could get synced and hear everything from the Hive. But that wasn't how it worked. He was a pilot, an exceptional one, and *listening to Hive chatter* wasn't his job.

Angh had looked at me like that. Looked at me as if he couldn't believe I was there, that he'd gotten me beneath him, that I was the very center of his world. No, of his whole universe. At least, I'd thought so in the moment.

But that could have been orgasm induced hallucinations.

"I will contact Doctor Helion and ask for another member of the team to assist on the next mission," Vice Admiral Niobe said. She was out of her gear and stacking it neatly for the clean-up crew waiting off to the side. They would search and scan the shuttle for Hive tech and make sure it was ready to go out again. A critical job since we would go out again. And again.

Unless we found a way to destroy this Hive mine network, we'd never regain the ground lost in this sector. The two mining planets, Latiri 4 and Latiri 7, were still active battlegrounds. The Coalition Fleet had been forced to retreat when the explosive weapons were first deployed more than two years ago. We'd gone from a firm foothold in this sector to nearly losing it in a matter of hours.

But Commander Phan had saved the entire battlegroup. Hell, the entire war, as far as I was concerned. And although we both had the experimental Hive tech implants in our heads, for some reason, she could hear the mines *talking* to one another, and I could not. I could hear the Hive Soldiers. The Scouts. But not their ships or their mines.

Which made me feel pretty fucking useless right now.

Doctor Helion, the Prillon warrior in charge of the experimental brain tech for the I.C., was working on a fix, but at the moment, it seemed there was no logical explanation for hers to work and for mine to fail, beyond basic biological differences in the way her brain was wired.

Since every single brain was unique, the doctor didn't know who would be able to hear them, and who would not. Who would amplify the sound for someone else. Apparently, for Chloe Phan, that someone wasn't me.

"That's great, Vice Admiral, but the solution to this problem is sitting on The Colony right now, bored out of his fucking mind," Chloe said. She still had the snap to her voice of a frustrated fighter, but it was laced with respect. "I didn't stay here for my health. I was going to retire, go live the quiet life on Prillon Prime. But Commander Karter asked us to stay, so we stayed. And now I'm telling you, we need Warlord Anghar."

Niobe watched Chloe stack her armor and helmet with intense interest. Thank God, because they both missed my gut wrenching reaction to hearing Angh's name come from another woman. My heart skipped a beat as I knew I'd heard her correctly. Chloe knew Angh?

"Tell me about the Atlan. He's contaminated?" Niobe asked. "How bad is it?"

Chloe sighed. "With all due respect Vice Admiral, he's

a decorated Warlord who survived being captured by the Hive. His level of contamination should be asked at about the same time you want to know his shoe size."

I agreed with Chloe, pleased that she'd defended the Atlan.

The Coalition's obsession with the idea of their warriors being *contaminated* once they'd been captured by the Hive didn't sit well with most humans. But then, we were new to the war. The other Coalition planets had been fighting for hundreds of years.

When Vice Admiral Niobe only dipped her head in understanding of her error, Chloe continued. "Yes, he's on The Colony. He survived months as a Drone until Captain Mills freed him on a ReCon mission. Months, sir. He's the strongest person I know, and not because he's an Atlan." Chloe lowered her chin slightly and raised her hand to point to her temple. "In here. He's a tough fucking bastard, and the most honorable Warlord, warrior or fighter I've ever met. We need him out here. I don't care what the rest of the Coalition thinks. He helped me save the Sector once. I see no reason he shouldn't help us do it again."

"How?" I asked. The word blurted from me before I could stop it. This was something I didn't know about the Warlord whom I suspected I was falling in love with. That was an insane notion, since I'd only spent one night with him, but my lingering reaction to him was far from normal. My body literally ached for him, and from him. My pussy was sore and if anyone got sight of me naked, they'd see the hickeys and other marks of our wild lovemaking.

Discovering more about his past wasn't helping in that

regard. I only liked him more and more. He wasn't just a quick lay now. He was a decorated, revered and qualified Warlord. If Chloe vouched for him, then he'd earned her respect. The hard way.

"How did he help you?" I asked. "He was here?"

Vice Admiral Niobe noticed my interest, her gaze narrowing on me as if she could somehow know I'd spent time in his bed on The Colony just the night before. She knew what was happening at the Academy, but I wasn't sure if she knew I'd been the one to lead the training exercise on that planet.

"Do you know Warlord Anghar?" she asked.

I nodded. "Yes. I just met him during the last training run on The Colony." I wouldn't lie, but I could leave out the part where I'd sat on his face and he'd made me come with his tongue.

"That was less than two days ago."

I nodded, wiped my hair back from my face. "Correct. I spoke with him briefly hours before I left." And fucked him. And screamed his name. And rode his cock until I dropped into blissful exhaustion. But she didn't need to know any of that. Good thing, because Chloe moved so she was in my face.

"How is he?" she asked, her voice full of friendly worry. "I haven't seen him for almost two years."

Jealousy reared its ugly head, but I knew Chloe was mated. Very well mated, if the prowling Prillon pilot was any indication. I'd heard she'd had a baby, took the requisite leave for that. She wasn't having a baby with the Prillon and Earth mate while secretly lusting after Angh. But jealous thoughts were irrational ones and I shook the feeling off.

Chloe's question didn't seem to bother her mate in the slightest. No jealousy there.

I shrugged. "He's fine, I guess. He was fighting in the pits when I met him." I glanced at Captain Dorian Zanakar. "Knocked out a Prillon warrior with one punch to the jaw."

Dorian burst out laughing. "That sounds about right. If there's something he wants, he goes for it, even if that's winning."

The *something* he'd wanted was me. I just nodded my head in neutral agreement.

Chloe's smile was filled with relief and she stepped back, finally allowing her mate to wrap an arm around her waist as she looked at the Vice Admiral. "We need to get him back out here. He helped me destroy the initial network. We need people who can hear those things, and he can hear them. Trust me."

Vice Admiral Niobe looked to me. "You spoke to him. Do you feel he is stable enough to handle this type of assignment? He is an Atlan. If there's any chance he is in danger of losing control to Mating Fever, I'd rather know now. The last thing I need is an out of control Atlan beast with Cyborg-enhanced strength."

All eyes turned to me and I thought of Angh. Was he in control? And what, exactly, was this *Mating Fever* she was talking about? He hadn't been in any kind of sickness or distress when he'd been with me. He'd been wild, admitted his beast was on the prowl, but that was all because he was horny, not sick. And I'd sated both him and his beast. He hadn't had any kind of fever when I'd slipped from his bed.

"He's strong, as Commander Phan said," I confirmed.

"I didn't see any sign of distress or illness. If we need him to help us destroy the Hive network in this sector, I don't see any reason not to use him."

And maybe, just maybe, I'd get to see him again.

The Vice Admiral nodded, her decision made. "Very well, Commander." She turned to Chloe. "I will request he be transferred to I.C. Core Command upon my return to Zioria."

"Thank God." Chloe leaned into Dorian's embrace and I was struck by an odd lump in my throat. Those two were so natural with one another. So trusting. There was something there I couldn't explain or completely believe was real, but I wanted it for myself. The whole *mates* thing —connecting on the deepest of levels...everywhere— wasn't something I fully understood. But I ached for the connection Chloe and Dorian shared. And I imagined the bond was even more intense when their other mate was with them.

I wanted that. I wanted that with Angh. My Atlan. My beast. The idea of him holding any other woman that way made my body scream in denial. Made me want to go all beast mode myself.

But if he got transferred to the I.C., they would send him all over the galaxy. The Hive deployments of this new weapon were increasing steadily, more and more battlegroups struggling to hold the front lines in this crazy war.

I wanted him. He wanted me. I knew that. The mating cuffs he'd placed on my chest had been a pretty damn clear invitation. But neither one of us was free to fall in love. *He* was, but he needed his mate to live on The Colony with him and I couldn't do that. I couldn't fall in love with a Colony Warlord. The Vice Admiral was fairly...flexible, but I doubted *that* flexible.

We were fighting a bigger battle than the one with our hearts. I had foolishly believed that the Coalition needed me. They did. But the truth was that the Coalition needed both of us. They needed Angh, but had somehow overlooked him and his abilities. Left him to live out a bland, less-useful existence on The Colony. Billions of lives depended on those like us to *listen* to the Hive and help find a way to win this war. And if that meant we couldn't be together, so be it. I'd walked away from him because of my job with the I.C. The depressing truth was that I'd never had him to begin with.

We both had a job to do. If he'd still have me, we'd just have to steal our pleasure where we could. Find moments to be together and kiss one another goodbye. Every single mission was dangerous. There was no guarantee either one of us would come back alive. Yet I longed for him, for whatever touches, kisses and hugs I could get.

"Mommy!" The high-pitched squeal was so out of place on the huge battleship that I jumped. A toddler with her mother's green eyes and dark black hair was running full speed at Chloe, her arms wide open and joy on her little face. She looked like she wasn't yet two, her chubby cheeks more baby than young girl, and her adorable little legs pumping as fast as they could, which wasn't fast at all. And quite clumsy. I worried she would trip and fall before she got close.

Chloe's entire demeanor changed at the voice, the fierce warrior replaced by a doting mother in an instant. She picked up the little girl and hugged her tightly, covering her daughter's soft cheeks with dozens of kisses as the girl chanted, "Mommy, Mommy, Mommy."

All work in the shuttle bay stopped as war-hardened warriors turned to watch the spectacle. Dorian snuggled in close and picked up the girl's tiny hand to place kisses on her palm. "What about your papa, Dara? I need kisses, too."

The little one laughed and held out her arms to Dorian, who pulled her from her mother's embrace and smothered his daughter with kisses and tickles until she was squealing once again. Chloe's smile was indulgent, her stance relaxed as Captain Seth Mills, her human mate, walked forward and pulled her into his arms for a scorching hot kiss.

Whoa. Dominant, alpha male testosterone made my whole body go on simmer as I watched her melt into his arms.

She might be the ranking officer of the trio, but it was more than clear that she happily submitted to her mates in the bedroom. And the golden collars around all three of their necks? It wasn't exactly a wedding ring, but it was a blatant and obvious claiming. These three were mates, a family. They were never alone. Never lonely. Never lost.

Chloe pulled away, her breathing noticeably faster than it had been before the kiss. "Where's the baby?"

Seth smiled down at her. "Don't worry, tiger-mama. He's taking a nap in the nursery. But this one—" He nodded his chin in their daughter's direction. "—was with Commander Karter, monitoring the mission comms. When she heard that your shuttle was back, she was done being patient."

"I told you I don't want her in there," Chloe chided. "She understands what they are saying, Seth."

"I love Mander, Mommy."

Chloe was glowing, her love for that little girl lighting up her face. "I know you do, baby. Commander Karter loves you too, but that's a place for grow-ups. Not little girls."

She pouted and tapped her ears. "I hear you. I like to hear you."

Chloe sighed and shook her head, staring up at Dorian for help. "You approve of this? She's not even two yet."

"This is war, love," he replied gently. "She's safe and protected with the Commander. With everyone on the ship. If it gets too intense, he'll protect her. But we can't lie to her either. This is our life, the life we chose. We can't change things now."

"I know. I just wish we could end this damn war!" She was fuming again and I felt like I was riding the emotional rollercoaster with her just watching. Listening to them.

"No bad words, Mommy. You get spanking now." Dara was practically squirming with delight at the idea.

"Yes, she does." Seth's voice was full of heat, and my pussy clenched with need as I saw Chloe meet his gaze and lick her lips in challenge.

God help me, things were going to be hot as hell in their quarters after the kids' bedtime.

That made me want Angh even more. God, did I miss that damn Atlan.

Seth broke eye contact and looked at his daughter again. "When Dara heard you were here, she squirmed off Karter's lap and starting running." His smile was all proud papa. "Didn't you, baby?"

"Dada can't catch me." Dara said, making Dorian laugh.

"That's because your dada is slow, but your papa is fast," Dorian added.

"Chase me!" She wriggled in her father's hold. That fast, her greetings were over and she wanted to play. Dorian chuckled but set his daughter on her feet and granted her wish, chasing her—but never catching her— as she ran and played and squealed through the shuttle bay. Half a dozen grinning warriors watched out for her, moving boxes with sharp corners and anything she might trip over before she even got close. She was obviously well loved and very well protected by everyone on the ship. A pang of envy worked its way through my chest until it ached.

I'd given up on the idea of a family, of a real home, when I joined the I.C. But here was Chloe Phan, an active duty commander who'd been sent back to Earth in shame just a few years ago, volunteered to be an Interstellar Bride so she could return to space and now living a life I could only dream about.

How the hell had she pulled that off? Was this kind of match solely for those matched through the Brides Program?

"Shall we, Captain?" The feminine voice came from behind me. I'd all but forgotten that Vice Admiral Niobe was standing there, most likely not missing how I was practically ogling the mated trio and their daughter. "You have a battle sim to run in just a few hours. If we head to transport now, we can still make it back to Zioria so you aren't late."

I blinked, got my feet moving. "Yes. Of course." The Vice Admiral was not a fan of tardiness or excuses.

I was not going to stand here and moon over Chloe and her perfect family. Two hot warrior mates, still making a difference in the war, a beautiful daughter and a baby boy I'd yet to meet sleeping peacefully in a nursery somewhere on the ship.

They were the reason we had to take down the Hive space-mines. Them, and a thousand families like them on the battlegroups, and millions—*billions*—of families on the Coalition worlds.

As I followed the Vice Admiral back to transport, I swallowed over a lump of cold, hard facts. The Coalition needed Angh a lot more than I did. Families like Chloe's would be saved by his efforts. Efforts that had nothing to do with me. My heart was screaming for all or nothing, and it sure hurt like a bitch to realize I might get him here and there for a quickie, but that wouldn't be enough.

I truly would have to let him go.

$\mathcal{K}$*ira, Classroom 731-D, Coalition Academy, Zioria*

"—AND SO THE NEED TO HAVE TWO TEAMS INFILTRATE FROM opposite flanks simultaneously can limit casualties, confuse the Hive and allow for a remote transport point to be set up on the far side."

I pointed to a vid display that took up the wall of the classroom, the graphics that were shown moved to match my words. The combination of audio and visual learning was backed up with afternoon practical scenarios on the tactical training outdoor simulator. That would take place after lunch.

While I'd missed the first lecture this morning and another instructor had filled in for me, my team was ready to test their knowledge. It wasn't the same as the off-site training, not as intense or terrifying as the deep cave battle sims we ran on The Colony, but these worked.

Got their feet wet. Many of the cadets would fail this afternoon, but they'd be able to work with their teammates and run the simulations over and over again in their free time until their teams successfully survived the simulated op.

Since it was the first day of this practical, I only expected a few to succeed. The cadets had learned that the first day meant—typically—failing, which was a lesson in itself. Battle never went as planned. I'd learned that the hard way, and been painfully reminded of that fact on Battleship Karter just a few hours ago.

The reason I'd been on that mission was to act as a signal boost for Commander Phan, to help take down another Hive mine network. And I'd failed. My cranial implant had not synched with Chloe's. We'd both been flying blind out there in our space suits, praying for a breakthrough when all we could see before us was black space. We knew the mines were there. We just couldn't *find* them.

And so I was tired. My eyes were dry, almost gritty feeling, as if I'd been in a desert instead of on a battleship. My body was weary, all but begging me to sleep. I'd gone to my quarters, showered and changed into my instructor's uniform—my I.C. garb was a dirty, torn pile on the floor of my quarters. I'd looked at my bed, then the time, and skipped my bed for the second half of the morning curriculum.

The Vice Admiral was adamant that our missions not disturb the classroom schedule any more than necessary. And if that meant going to work feeling like I'd been run over by a tank...well, that was part of the job. No one could know just how many I.C. operatives were on Zioria.

The Academy the perfect cover. As long as none of us messed it up.

People noticed I missed a class now and then—they'd have to be blind, and idiots, not to—but working for the I.C. required my disappearance at random times, top secret clearance and an ability to live a double life.

Right now, I was on perma-loan to Commander Phan's squadron stationed on Battleship Karter. But that might be a thing of the past.

They'd want Warlord Anghar now. I hoped they would keep me in the loop, let me try to help because I really, really wanted an excuse to see him again, and I didn't want to have to wait until the end of the next student quarter when we took the next graduation class there for battle sims.

That was *months* away. And judging by the obsessive nature of my thoughts, and the almost debilitating desire I had to curl into a ball next to him in bed and beg him to hold me as I slept, that was too long. Way too long.

I answered student questions and ignored the way my body ached, and it wasn't just from the mission. That had been nothing. No, this ache was from the wild night with Angh. God, that had been...hot. Insane. Amazing. Melody had been right; I'd needed to get laid. And now that I'd had a hot Atlan and his beast, I was pretty much ruined for any other male. In. The. Universe.

He'd practically frazzled my brain cells with the orgasms. The guy was *good.* The sex, intense. He'd called me mate, put his Atlan cuffs on. He'd spouted almost-romance and I'd been too drugged up on endorphins and all the other chemicals released in my body from orgasm overload to process everything he was saying. No, not overload. That would mean what he'd done to me was enough. More than enough.

I could *never* come too much where that smoking hot Atlan was concerned. I wondered if he'd be around on my next trip to Battlegroup Karter. Maybe I could talk the Vice Admiral into some time off, and Angh into a repeat performance. Fun for both of us, two consenting adults having wild monkey sex. All. Night. Long.

My pussy clenched with heat at the very idea. I would check the training calendar as soon as class got out and make sure my name was on the instructor roster for the next Colony run as well. If I had to wait months, then I had to wait. But at least I had a guaranteed way to see him again. Normally, we instructors did our best to avoid traveling to The Colony, trading favors and committing everything up to and including bribery to avoid the three days of dark cave training. But now? If I knew that beast was waiting for me, I'd volunteer every damn time.

But that was crazy thinking. It had just been one night. One night to pull out my wild side, let my inhibitions drop to the floor beside my clothes and let a beast take control. It had been hot and crazy and totally wild. But it was just one night.

The Earth saying, 'That guy was a beast in the bedroom,' really was the truth. I'd just had to travel a galaxy away to prove it. I doubted any of my Earth friends would believe me, besides Melody. She'd been giving me looks all morning from her desk. I knew I'd have to spill all the steamy details after-hours. If I could stay awake that long. I needed a ReGen wand for my pussy...and my brain.

I cleared my throat. "Any more questions?" I asked,

trying to keep my mind on the topic, not how big an Atlan's cock was in beast mode.

Gah! Focus.

The room reminded me of a typical college classroom on Earth. Movie theater style, with each row being tiered up so the vid wall—okay, not part of an Earth college classroom—could be seen from their desks. Windows overlooking the outdoor simulation area were along one side, and the Academy hallway on the other, but the windows were tinted dark for the lecture. No one could see in or out.

The theater seating also reminded me of the fighting pit on The Colony, although that had been in a semi-circle, almost gladiator style. I remembered the movie about the gladiator, the one with the hot movie star... Australian, maybe? I'd thought he'd been gorgeous, all ripped muscles and male intensity. But Angh had him beat. He was bigger, badder and the testosterone that Atlan oozed had ruined my panties.

Even now, hours later, my nipples got hard just thinking about him. And as for wet panties, mine were *still* ruined. Every time I thought about Angh, which was about every other minute, my panties got another dose of lust. If it weren't for the birth control shot I took, I'd be in a panic right now, not just under-slept and over-sexed.

A cadet from Viken called out. "Instructor Dahl, how will those who set up the transport area be able to go ahead?"

I walked to the right side of the vid wall, pressed a button on the remote I held. The simulation started at the beginning and I began to explain how the transport group would be coming in behind the two teams to capture the enemy base and set up a transport zone. That would be a mine team, and the job in a real battle was both risky and dangerous. I paused the display at the spot I was looking for to answer his question, walked so I could point right at a specific spot.

"There. We'll take high ground. That's the vantage point we need to take out their rear guard and—"

A huge bang startled everyone. I stopped talking, heads swiveled to the classroom door.

Another loud banging sounded from the closed door, as if someone wasn't just knocking, but pounding. I didn't have a weapon, neither did any of the cadets. Weapons were for the outdoor training simulator or the other building where classes on that topic were held. The building alarm was silent. The comms unit on my wrist had no alerts—and I'd had them come through in the past for random emergency drills—and they had woken me from a sound sleep. This was something else.

I walked toward the door, watched the knob rattle. I held up my hand as some cadets stood, ready to do... something. We didn't even know what the threat was yet.

I pressed the button on the remote, the windows going transparent, the room brightening. If there was a threat, I wanted to be able to see it.

The door opened—this wasn't a sliding door like on a spacecraft, but a door just like they had on Earth. With the sound of rending metal, the door was ripped from the hinges. I didn't even get a chance to step close because in stormed Angh, holding the door in his hand. He still gripped the knob, the metal bent, the hinges shredded as if made of tin foil.

I sucked in a breath as his gaze roved over the room

for a brief second then landed on me. He was breathing hard, as if he'd been in a fighting pit. I recognized he was partially transformed into beast mode, huge, but not enormous. His hair was wild, his uniform pristine. The cuffs glinted. Not just the ones about his wrists, but the ones he'd laid on my bare chest the other night, the ones he'd wanted for me. They hung from his belt like bells, clanging together in my ears. The slight tinkling music was, for me, loud as cannon fire.

He said nothing, but he didn't have to. He was here for me.

Holy shit.

My lady parts perked up at his presence, although I was too tired to go another round. Knowing how Angh liked to fuck, I needed more than a nap. I needed to eat my Wheaties first.

He was more attractive than I remembered. Bigger. More powerful. More intense. My heart rate kicked up, my palms were damp. *Other* places were damp as well. My body *knew* him and wanted him. I wanted to jump into his arms and have him spin us about so I was pressed against the wall again. Crazy thoughts for a crazy situation.

I vaguely noticed a man following him, but when he slapped his hand on Angh's shoulder, I couldn't miss him. He was human. Dark skinned, dark hair, dark uniform. Everything on him was dark. Like a six-foot tall chocolate mocha.

"Dude, you could have just opened the door." He shook his head and if he didn't have silver, Hive integrated eyes, he probably would have rolled them.

Dude? I hadn't heard that expression since Earth. Angh's sidekick was human. African-American, based on the accent. And from the South. I looked at him. "You from the South?"

"Atlanta, Georgia." He bowed low and Melody stepped forward.

"I'm from Berlin. Germany." Her voice was a bit higher than normal and I turned my head to narrow my eyes at her in warning. She ignored me, of course, and kept talking. "I saw you. On The Colony. I didn't know they had any humans there. Except the mates of course." She flipped her hair and smiled. A really big, come and get me, smile. I so did not need this right now. One set of female hormones getting us in trouble was enough.

And I was in deep fucking trouble if the Atlan with the heaving chest was any indication.

Angh just stared and breathed. Hard.

The human gripped the door by the side and tugged. Angh finally let it go and I was shocked when the much smaller human man took the door like it weighed nothing more than a piece of driftwood and tossed it into the hallway.

"Do you want me to notify security?" a male cadet asked, although I didn't turn my head to see who it was.

I shook my head. "Yes, although not because there is a threat. Notify them that everything is fine. I'm sure the door alarm was triggered."

"But—"

"Stand down, Cadet," I replied in the voice I usually used outdoors in the training simulator.

The whispering began then. The murmurs. *This* was going to be talked about. Forever.

7

*K*ira

I FLICKED MY GAZE TO MELODY AS SHE CAME TO STAND beside me. "Um, Instructor Dahl…"

She used my title since we were in the classroom, but I knew she wanted to say *What the fuck, girlfriend? The hot Atlan beast you fucked just came to Zioria and ripped a door off your classroom to get to you.*

"If he's going to make an ass of himself, that's fine. I'm guessing you're Instructor Kira Dahl." Sidekick stepped forward, held out his hand in typical Earth greeting, a handshake. "I'm Denzel. Lieutenant Denzel Washington."

I looked over his shoulder at Angh, then met Denzel's silvery gaze.

Melody snickered beside me. "Denzel Washington? Really?"

Denzel's cyborg eyes shifted to her and I would swear

they both stopped breathing. After a long, awkward silence, he grinned. "Only a human would find my name humorous." While he'd been easy-going before, his entire expression changed. He was completely opposite of Angh. Calm, cool and collected. "Yes, my grandmother had a crush on the actor and we just happened to have the same last name. I was doomed."

"Doomed?" Melody asked. "You're looking pretty good for a doomed man."

I couldn't miss the flirting tone from Melody or the look of interest on the lieutenant's face. Or my cadets. Every cadet in the room was craning to get a better view. And I soooo did not need this kind of gossip flying around the campus. I'd have ten different nicknames by this time tomorrow.

"Class dismissed," I called. "Be ready for the battle sim after lunch."

The group didn't need to be told twice. Their whispers rose to full conversations as they practically ran out the doors, more than likely ready to spread all kinds of stories.

Denzel was staring at Melody and when I turned my head to look at her, *she* was staring at him. She was beautiful. I had to respect his interest. She was tall and lithe with mahogany hair that fell to her waist and bedroom eyes, dark brown and eating him up like he was her favorite dessert. Neither of them spoke another word.

All righty then.

I moved out of their way and walked over to Angh. It wasn't as if I could avoid him. I certainly didn't want to walk out of the room and move any possible scene elsewhere in the building.

"What are you doing here?" I asked. I had to tilt my head back, *way back*, to look at him. His breathing hadn't slowed. The lips I'd kissed—a lot—were parted. His cheeks were flushed as if he had a fever, his muscles all but rippling as he eyed me. As if I were prey. *This* was how he'd looked at me as he'd curled his finger, beckoned me to his side at the fighting pit.

My eagerness for him hadn't waned. After a night with him, my libido kicked right back into gear and I wanted him, too.

"I'm here for you," he said, his voice deep. He wasn't in beast mode, since he said more than one word, but it seemed it lurked right beneath the surface. "You left with no explanation, Kira. Not even a goodbye."

I nodded, licked my lips and his eyes dropped to my mouth. "I'm sorry. My transport was scheduled first thing and I didn't want to wake you." Lame answer, but the truth. When he just stared, not saying a word, I kept babbling. "I figured you were tired after...you know."

His gaze darkened and I could feel the heat pouring off him like a blast furnace. He was thinking about fucking me now. And I was thinking about his cock, and his mouth, and...everything else.

Great. My cheeks were so hot they were probably the color of maraschino cherries.

"Get out." He spoke to Denzel and Melody, but his gaze hadn't left me.

Denzel took Melody by the elbow, escorting her to the doorway with a protective—and possessive—hand at the small of her back. But she twisted in his hold, craning her neck to check on me. "You okay with this, Dahl? I can call security."

I looked up at Angh, at the anguish I could now see in the lines of strain around his eyes and mouth. He was holding on by a very thin thread. I'd hurt him somehow— I wasn't quite sure what this was yet—but I knew he wouldn't harm me. Never. "Go on, Mel." I looked deeply into Angh's eyes. "He would never hurt me."

"Never." The Warlord confirmed. With a shrug, Melody returned her attention to Denzel.

"What is going on?" Melody asked him. "What are you two doing here?"

"Let's go somewhere quiet so we can talk about that... and other things."

With every courtesy, Denzel led her to the hallway, lifted the door from the floor and set it back in place the best he could.

We had the illusion of privacy, at least. The display screen windows were still clear, and we were gathering a crowd in the hallway on the other side of the glass.

With a sigh, I moved to the wall control and blackened the screens once more. I had no idea what was about to happen with Angh, but I knew I didn't need an audience.

That done, I walked back to the Atlan, who stood in the exact place he'd been when he first saw me, as if he were an oak tree and his roots were so deep they touched the core of the world.

"What are you doing here?" I asked, repeating Melody's question.

He growled, eyes narrowed, and lifted his hand to crook a finger at me, just like he'd done at the arena. "Come here, mate."

And just like that, I couldn't deny him or myself. I wanted to feel his arms around me almost as much as I wanted to breathe. I'd missed him and the longing erupting within me was strange and alarming.

I closed the distance, pressing my face to his chest and wrapping my arms around his waist as his giant hands settled on my back, stroking up and down. He bent low and buried his nose in my hair.

He stiffened. "Why do I smell Prillon blood in your hair? And ion blaster fire?" He dropped to his knees, not to talk to me, but to personally check every inch of my body for injury, starting at the ankles and working his way up. While his hands on me were clinical, I felt the touch everywhere. "Tell my why you smell of another male's blood, mate, or I will not be able to control my beast."

"Angh!" I pushed at his hands as they squeezed and worked my thighs, my ass, pressed on my abdomen, felt my breasts, not with seduction in mind, but the single-minded intention of uncovering any hurt. Did he really think my boobs were broken?

When he got to my right elbow, I winced. I couldn't help it. He froze, his gaze lifting to mine. "You are injured. This is unacceptable."

"I'm fine." I was. It was sore, but it would heal, just like every other scrape or bruise, ache or pain I got from one of my missions. I'd had much worse.

"Who hurt you, Kira? Tell me his name and I will destroy him."

Oh boy, I needed reminding as to why overprotective, dominant males were a bad idea for a one-night stand? Oh, yeah. This. So much this. Besides ripping my classroom door off, he looked like I'd struck him through the heart, like the bruise on my arm from the asshole Hive

—whose hard as steel kick I'd blocked with my elbow right before I shot him through the heart—was the most important thing in the universe. He happened to be a former Prillon warrior and his blood had splattered all over my armored suit. Which meant my quarters probably smelled like his blood, too. Which was just freaking fantastic.

"He's already dead, Angh. It's nothing. A bruise."

He didn't seem mollified by my answer. "Why did you not seek medical attention?"

"It's nothing." I didn't dare tell him why I hadn't gone to the med station, and not just because I hadn't had time. If I went in, they'd have put me in a ReGen pod, and the sore, very satisfied feeling in my pussy, my physical reminder of him, of our wild night together, would be gone forever. I *wanted* to know he'd possessed me completely, filled me up. Made me scream. The tenderness between my legs was my personal, very private souvenir of our time together. I wanted more, had a feeling I would *always* want more when it came to this very sexy Atlan, but I had a job to do. I'd made promises. Signed contracts.

I wasn't in a place to start a relationship right now. The I.C. owned me for two more years. Every mission saved lives, sometimes one, sometimes a hundred. I couldn't be selfish. My pussy was not in charge of this situation, no matter how badly my body was screaming at me to strip off my clothes and beg him to fuck me again. Right now. Up against the wall. On the desk. Even the hard floor.

But I'd only be making things worse if I did that. Whatever this was, it had to end. My commanding officer in the I.C. would *not* be amused by the fact that I'd fucked an Atlan in the first place, and on a training trip. But *mating* one? They'd probably throw me in the brig. They made it very clear on a previous mission that there was no getting out of my service, and I didn't want to. I saved lives. A lot of lives. And so would he, once the Vice Admiral got her claws into him. The warriors and civilians captured and tortured by the Hive needed me more than this Atlan did, more than I needed to feed the lust driving my libido to the next level whenever I looked at Angh. And the war needed him, my big, bad-ass beast.

Fighting for patience, and control, I placed my hands on his cheeks and lifted his face up so he would look at me. For once, he was shorter than me. Barely, though, even though he was on his knees. "Angh, why are you here? Why did you kick down my classroom door?"

"You are my mate, Kira."

He meant it. Shit. He believed it, transported to a different planet, broke down my door to tell me that. To come for me. The Everians with their marks weren't the only insane ones out there. I now realized an Atlan and his beast were doubly crazy.

"I'm not," I countered, shaking my head. "We had one great night. One unbelievable, hot night, but I can't be your mate. We weren't matched. I'm not an Interstellar Bride. I know you were tested."

God help my stupid, idiotic brain. Last night, before I went on the mission, I'd tortured myself by using my high-level security clearance to look him up in the database. "You have a perfect, matched mate out there who could be linked to you tomorrow. And I can't leave the Academy." I put a hand on my chest, then on his. "You can't leave The Colony. We live on two different worlds. We're *from* two different worlds."

"You will return with me to The Colony," he said, his tone fierce. "We will live there. Raise our children. You are mine, Kira. And I am yours. I do not want an Interstellar Bride. I want *you*. I wear your claim. I will pledge myself to you, only you. You own me already, mate. I am yours." He lifted his hands, showing me the cuffs that remained locked around his wrists.

He wasn't growling or talking in single word sentences. He was in control, not his beast. Yes, the sex had been great. Amazing. Fucking fantastic. But we'd never talked about me being his *mate*. As in forever. "No. I'm not your mate. I can't be."

With a sigh so deep his entire body shuddered, he leaned forward, his forehead pressed between my breasts. Breathed, held on. When he lifted his face, he was smiling. "All right, Kira. I will return to The Colony. But I would ask for one thing before I go."

"Anything." It was a vow. Anything I could give him, I would. Except being his mate. I *wished* I could give him myself, but that was impossible. I belonged to the I.C., a tangible thing that was their property, just like an ion blaster or a desk. I was a piece of equipment used to fight the Hive and they were far from done with me. Or him.

Angh belonged to the I.C. now, and someday, to some lucky bride who would be his perfect match. He deserved that. A woman who could stay by his side and be content —and she would be content with the way he wielded his cock as if it were a magic wand. He deserved a mate without torn loyalties. A woman who could be with him every day, every night, raise his children, and not torment herself with the body count of unsaved thousands. I couldn't walk away from my job with the I.C. no matter how much I wanted him.

"One more unbelievable, hot night of mindless fucking," he said.

He threw my own words back at me and my pussy went from hot to inferno in the space of a heartbeat. My nipples hardened, my panties ruined. My need for him was even greater than the first time I saw him in the fighting pit. I now knew who he was, what he was and how *skilled* he was. And all of that was focused right on me. Every virile, sexy inch of him. And there were *a lot* of inches. All over.

"Yes." I leaned over and kissed him, but tore my lips from his when it went hot and carnal in three seconds flat. I was already breathing hard as if I were outside in the outdoor training center and not inside with just his very skilled tongue making my knees buckle. "But not right now. I have to be on the training field in fifteen minutes for an instructors meeting."

"I want more than fifteen minutes." He lowered his hands to cup my ass and pulled me forward so I could feel the hard length of his swollen cock. Every hot inch of him.

"So do I. That's why we can't start now." I kissed him again because I had to. He was my kryptonite. There was no resistance in me. None. Not when his big hands were on me, his taste was in my mouth, the feel of him was against me.

"How long does this training take?" he asked.

"A couple hours." I could, perhaps, slip out early, but

after the door ripping incident, probably not. "Then I'll hit the showers, and I'll be all yours."

He stood without a word and let me go. All at once, I felt cold. Alone. He walked to the door and lifted it to the side so it was propped against the wall. "For one night."

Nodding, I walked through the doorway ahead of him. "Yes. For one night."

By now, the hallway was deserted. Thankfully. I didn't see Melody or Denzel, but they could take care of themselves.

"It will be worth it."

I meant to ask him what that meant, but the late-morning bell rang and the hallway quickly swarmed with cadets, going to their next class or practical session elsewhere on campus.

He stepped close, then leaned down so he could be heard. "What we did the other night, mate, was nothing."

Oh shit. Any better than before and I would die of pleasure.

8

A ngh

THE CADETS SWARMED THE GROUNDS BELOW LIKE AN ARMY of insects. I stood next to the Academy training commander and watched the activity from an observation deck. On the rocky terrain below was a mock battlefield eerily similar to the ground I'd fought for on Latiri 4, before we lost it to the Hive. Before I lost everything to the Hive.

Battlegroup Karter had been forced to retreat from the planet, and its twin, Latiri 7, when the strange new Hive weapon had been deployed. With Commander Phan, we'd managed to save the battlegroup, and I'd read reports that my old shipmates were steadily gaining ground in the sector once again. Most of that gain was due to the skills and talents of Commander Phan from Earth, and the strange Hive implant in her head.

We'd been the only two who could hear them. The enemy. And although we'd managed to dismantle their offensive net of explosives, her implant was put in place by the Intelligence Core. Mine was pure Hive. Just like the implants in my arms and back, my muscles.

I was contaminated. Commander Phan was not. And so she fought on with the Battlegroup while I'd been sent to The Colony to hope and pray to the gods for a mate, for some kind of decent life.

But even that would be denied me and I'd given up hope. Yet now—

"You have to tell her the truth. Tell her what will happen to you if she does not accept your claim." Denzel stood on my right, shoulder to shoulder, as we watched the battle scenario unfold below. Somewhere down there was my mate, directing her cadets in a mock battle that looked all too real. It set me on edge, my beast pacing, even though I knew it wasn't real. I'd seen real and didn't want to go back.

"Tell her the truth? I will not," I told him. "She has made her choice." I watched her move with a small strike team in a flanking maneuver. They hadn't been seen by their enemy combatants yet, and soon it would be too late for them to recover. In a short time, my mate would be upon them with her team and the game would be over.

Kira moved like a shadow, carried her weapon as if it were an extension of her arm. I only had eyes for her. Could pick her easily from a large crowd, or a mock battle. For others, she was obvious in her instructor's uniform, the others with her in the uniform of the cadet. she was easy to see. When she aimed her rifle, she did not miss, no matter the distance. The other instructors on the ground were skilled. Patient. But they didn't move as she did, like she was nothing more than a ghost passing through the darkness to destroy her enemies. It was obvious why she was an instructor. It was obvious she'd spent time in battle. She had stories I did not know, but I wanted to learn them all.

An unexpected sense of pride filled me as I watched her. She was a sight to behold. Beautiful and deadly. Fearless. She ducked an ion blast and didn't even pause in her step before returning fire and striking her 'enemy' down.

I knew the ion blasts were fake flashes of light, that the fallen were not truly dead, but the sights and sounds of battle were real, not forged. The screams of pain real as well, for the specialty training gear simulated the sting of taking an actual ion blast in armor if a cadet was hit. They had to be ready for anything, and being conditioned to deal with the jolt of an ion blast in a real battle could prove to be the difference between life and death.

Or worse. Turning into the likes of me.

I'd been through these simulations, this training. I'd been on that exact training field. There were no Atlans out there today, mostly the smaller races, those from Earth, Trion and Everis. I knew the Atlans and Prillon warriors trained for different types of missions, would use the field in different scenarios and practiced at a different time.

Below me, a pincer move-and-ambush on an enemy base camp was underway, led by my mate. The other three Academy commanders were pitted against her, their teams moving to protect the base flag that represented their stronghold.

Kira and her team were on high ground, moving to a flanking position as the rest of her team feigned a full-frontal assault. They struck hard and fast, then pulled back into a narrow ravine, taking up sniper positions to keep their enemies pinned down and engaged on their front line.

The Atlans were usually up front in a full ground assault, charging through the middle, tearing bodies in half as we went. The Prillons usually combined ground and air assault tactics, their pilots uncannily skilled at hitting targets on the ground with little to no margin for error.

But the stealth I witnessed here was astonishing.

"Damn, she's good." Denzel was watching as well, his arms crossed. He whistled when she moved directly behind the defending team's commander and took aim with her rifle. "She can't hit that shot. She's five hundred yards from the target."

The Academy observer snorted in disgust. He was a huge Prillon warrior, young, but strong. "Captain Dahl does not miss. Not from that short distance. I have seen her strike a Hive Scout through the heart from a mile away."

I grunted, but said nothing. A Hive Scout? What the fuck was my mate doing attacking a Hive Scout? But as the defender fell—from that substantial a shot—his body armor forcing him to remain unmoving on the ground, I watched Kira silently signal her team to move in on the flag target.

One by one her opponents fell. She struck in the rear, taking out the nearest defender until the opponents' entire team was focused forward and no one remained to defend their flank.

As she walked forward and lifted the flag from its base with no resistance, I realized that I had no idea what my mate was capable of. I knew little to nothing about her or her life. Her history. Her training. Her job here. I wanted her. Needed her. My beast howled for only her, yet there was much to learn. She was my very soul, yet a complete enigma.

I turned to the Prillon, who was grinning as the alarm bell rang, signaling a victor. "Hive Scout? Do the instructors here frequently go into enemy territory?" I had never head of such a thing, but I had to admit I did not know anything about the Coalition Academy or how it was operated. I had trained on Atlan, in a different facility before being voted in as commander of my unit. The election was a huge honor and I had served proudly up until the day I was captured by the Hive.

The Prillon cleared his throat, then turned to me with one eyebrow raised. "Apologies Warlord, did you ask me a question?"

I frowned. He'd heard me. We both knew it. "I asked, Prillon, if the instructors here normally go on strike missions against Hive positions? Do they go into active combat?"

He grinned. "Not normally. No. But Captain Dahl isn't exactly normal, is she?"

"Do all of your instructors hold the rank of Captain?"

"No. Of course not." Shaking his head like I was a fool, he turned from us and made his way down to the field. Victors and those who had been defeated now stood shoulder to shoulder on the ground as the Prillon recounted what he'd seen from his vantage point in the tower. Strengths. Weaknesses. Mistakes.

Through it all, my mate stood with the victory flag in one hand and her rifle in the other. She had removed her helmet and used the flag arm to hold it on her hip. Her hair was a wild, sweaty tangle and her eyes intense and focused with the challenge and victory, but not surprise. I saw no arrogance or excitement. Around her, chests heaved with exertion. Cadets threw up or dug at their uniforms, fighting the heat or resonant pain of the ion blasts they'd taken.

She looked unmoved. A stone statue. Calm. Calculating. Unmoved by the possibility of pain or even death.

I knew that look. I'd seen it in the mirror.

It was the look of an experienced warrior, not a teacher at the Academy. Not a female who worked in a classroom. She'd led her group through the exercise but it hadn't been one for her. She'd done this before and the ion blasts had been real.

She said she couldn't be mine, that she had a job to do.

Why did I now believe that my mate was keeping secrets from me? Even with a night so intimate, our darkest desires, our bodies completely exposed, I didn't know what was in her head.

I would have one night to learn everything. And I wanted to know *everything*. Every secret. Every place she liked to be touched. Every sound and scent and taste of her on my tongue. I wanted to know about her life, her past, her dreams for the future. I wanted a lifetime in one night. But I would take what I could get, the stolen moments of bliss, and then I would let her go. I'd have to. I had no choice.

Denzel tensed next to me as the female, Melody, pulled off her helmet as well. She was wincing, her arm wrapped around her side as if she'd taken a hit to the ribs.

"Go. See to your woman," I ordered.

"She's not mine."

It was my turn to cross my arms and look at another warrior as if he were an idiot. "So, you won't mind if that Trion male next to her helps her to medical, as he is offering to do?"

Denzel's head whipped around to check out the opposition. "Fuck that."

He took off at a run and I chuckled. At least one good thing would come of this trip. No, two good things. It seemed Denzel had found his mate, and I would spend one more night in heaven with mine.

"I'll meet you in transport at noon tomorrow," I called.

Denzel waved in acknowledgement and took off at a run for the mock battlefield, shoving people out of his way until he stood toe-to-toe with his female. She looked up at him, way up, and whatever he said, she smiled, placing her hand in his. He had a fucking way with the females.

Looked as if Denzel was going to be a happy man tonight, and I had every intention of being one, too. Kira's warm, wet pussy awaited. Her body. Her laughter. Her bed. *Everything.*

9

K̸ira, Private Quarters

I CLOSED MY EYES AS THE DRYING TUBE BLEW HOT AIR ALL over my body. It was like standing inside a hand dryer in the public restrooms on Earth. This was something I hadn't gotten used to, being put into a mini-hurricane instead of using a towel. I didn't mind today because I was in a rush.

Angh was in his quarters.

Waiting.

My heart skipped a beat and when the machine shut off, I took a deep breath, let it out. I was nervous, like a fifteen-year old girl with her first crush. But my body wasn't behaving like a teenager's. No, my reactions were all woman. My pussy still ached from our last time together, my nipples hardened remembering the feel of them in his mouth, the tug of suction he'd used, the sweet slide of his teeth over them. My back was bruised along my spine from being pressed against the wall, ruthlessly fucked with a desperation we'd both shared. The whisker burn on the inside of my thighs. The ruthless skill of his tongue.

I shuddered, my temperature felt like it jumped ten degrees.

My body remembered all of it, wanted him again. My brain wanted him, too, but knew it was a bad idea. Bad ideas sometimes felt really, really good and this was one of them.

One night.

He wanted one more night. So did I. I couldn't deny him, or myself.

Opening the door of the bathroom, I stepped out, saw Angh leaning against the wall just inside the doorway. Naked. Very naked and very, very erect. Why did he look *bigger* today? I couldn't believe that beast of a cock had fit inside me. It was porn star worthy. No wonder my pussy was sore. No wonder my body screamed *Yes! More!*

I froze, surprised, then instantly aroused. "I...I didn't know you were here."

The corner of his mouth turned up as his gaze traveled over my body, from the tips of my toes to the top of my head with pit stops at my breasts and my pussy. "The guest quarters are adequate, but not needed for more than the bathing tube. It is your bed I want to be in tonight, although I have no intention of sleeping."

I licked my lips. Sleep? Who needed sleep? Seeing him again, every bare, gorgeous inch of him, had me needy, and I knew I was going to be insatiable once I got my hands—and mouth—on him.

We just stood and stared. I took in his size, well over a foot taller than me. His hair was dark and a tad unruly and from the looks of it, a touch damp, as if he'd skipped the drying tube in his haste to get to me. His eyes were dark and brooding, as usual, but the heat in them, the need, was scorching. Whiskers darkened his square jaw and I wanted to feel the rasp of them against my skin again. His full lips were parted as if he was breathing hard. He was, because I watched his broad chest rise and fall. A smattering of dark hair covered his chest, specifically between his flat, dark nipples, then tapering to his navel. Below that, it went in a straight line down to the thatch of curls at the base of his cock.

But I'd skipped so much and had to backtrack to his broad shoulders, rippled and bulging with muscles. His corded forearms flexing and relaxing with each opening and closing of his fists. His washboard abs, narrow waist, lean hips. Then there was his cock, thick and long, capped with a broad head. The skin was smooth and taut, a pulsing vein ran up the length. Farther down, his legs were powerful, his thighs as wide as my waist. He was built like a tank, a gorgeous, mouth-watering tank.

But there was one thing—no, two things—I'd skipped over, two places too painful to linger. The cuffs on his wrists. Wide and silver-toned, they were carved with elegant marks. *His family's marks.* To him, the cuffs meant he was claimed. That he was mine. Of all the women in the galaxy, he'd chosen me.

That fact was humbling and frightening all at once, because I wasn't free to follow my heart. I'd signed a contract with the I.C., and no one just walked away. Not before their time was up. And not when there was still so much work to be done.

I could have Angh, but how many people would die because I was selfish? Because I wasn't strong enough to deny my heart the one thing it had every really wanted?

Him. My beast. He was mine. The truth was there, in his eyes, in the way he looked at me, like I was the only female in existence. I knew, in my soul, I knew he would fight for me. Kill for me. Die for me.

I just hadn't understood at the time, when he'd placed the cuffs on my chest. I had been too caught up in my body's needs, mindless with desire. To be with him, I wouldn't be walking away from a desk-job as an instructor of Planetary History or Interplanetary Species. Those had been my worst subjects at the Academy.

Now I realized just how much a bit of extra studying during my early days in the Fleet would have paid off. I would have recognized Angh's intent instantly, the depth of his desire for me. The gift he was offering me when we'd been together and he'd placed those cuffs on my chest.

A mate. A lifetime of absolute devotion and protection from one of the strongest, most honorable males I'd ever met.

He'd offered me the matching cuffs and I'd felt the cool weight of the metal when he'd set them on my heated skin. But not the weight of their meaning. I'd turned them down. I hadn't wanted jewelry from him. Couldn't wear it in my role. But it wasn't just jewelry. The cuffs were every bit as powerful as an Everian's mark. It was a claiming. A connection. An offer of forever.

The thought of what he wanted had me glancing away.

I wanted him. I did. My body screamed at me to close the distance between us, put my hands on him. Climb him like a monkey. Kiss him, lick him, sink down on his big cock. But I couldn't keep him. Not for more than tonight.

I'd signed my life away. Committed to a life of service to the Coalition Fleet, to the war, to protecting hundreds of planets and billions of innocent lives. Just as Angh had done when he'd joined his fellow Atlan warriors in fighting the Hive. I was human and I didn't have any of the *out clauses* that other species had. I didn't have any of the problems like those from other planets. Everians had a back-out clause if their mark awakened. Atlan Warlords would be sent to prison if they went into Mating Fever. Prillons could be separated from their mates, but their collars tied them together telepathically, which was pretty darn cool. And creepy. And the Prillons lived and died on their Battleships. Raised their families. Their females accepted two mates in case one of them was killed in battle.

That was what I'd learned about the other species and their customs. I was a battle commander. I led small strike squads of human, Trion and Viken warriors. We were not big enough for infantry battle, for facing the Hive Soldiers head-on in ground combat. That was left to the larger races, the Prillon and Atlan warriors, and a few others who were strong enough to lift a Hive off the ground and literally tear his body in two.

That I'd seen. *That* was something I knew about the Atlan warrior staring at me now like I was the most desirable creature he'd ever seen.

I wanted him. If I was completely honest with myself, I was already falling in love with him. And yet, I was stuck with my contract. I didn't have a special collar, or ancient mark that would spark to life and get me a *get out of jail free* card. I could meet a warrior like Angh and fall in love with him, but it could never be more than a quick, wild romp.

What the heck was I doing? Standing here, staring at a naked Atlan Warlord who blatantly wanted me, thinking of what I *couldn't* have when he was so blatantly offering me exactly what I wanted. Him. Naked. Right now.

"I'm not tired, Warlord," I finally said, agreeing with him that we wouldn't be getting much sleep tonight. If I had one night with him, if that's what he wanted, I wouldn't waste a second of it sleeping. I walked to him and he pushed off the wall, met me halfway.

His hand came up, brushed my hair back from my face, but didn't touch me. Only his cock made contact as it prodded my belly. For one so big, his touch was gentle. I felt so small, tiny, beside him. My eyes were level with his chest and I couldn't hold off any longer. I lifted my hand, placed it on his belly, watched as the muscles quivered, heard the way he inhaled a quick breath. It was like electricity, touching him again. A current of desire went through me, lightning-quick, right to my pussy. I clenched my inner muscles in anticipation. I could feel my nipples harden, ache. And that had been from a simple touch.

My hand slid left to right, my eyes following, seeing him and learning his body. A scar here, a flexing muscle there. I admired his physique, his perfection. I paid no special attention to the cyborg parts in his biceps, the faint glimmer of metal in the corded muscles of his neck and shoulders. He was magnificent, and all of that was simply part of him now, just like the other scars.

He didn't move to touch me, but his hands flexed open and closed as if it took all of his control not to. I tilted my head back, glanced up at him. Way up. His dark eyes met mine and I saw his heart in them. He hid nothing from me. He was raw and hurting. Not just the searing desire, but his need, his desperate and absolute devotion.

Looking into his eyes was the strongest aphrodisiac. I knew I was safe with him. Always. There was love in those dark depths, in the way he trembled, holding back as I touched him. He let me have my way, for now, and I knew by the shudders passing through his body how that control cost him. Yet he did it, for me.

"You're so damn beautiful." The confession poured out of me as I spread the fingers of both my hands, splayed them wide so I could make maximum contact with his skin. I parted my lips and his eyes lowered to them. That was it, a silent snap of the tension between us. It broke and so did his control. His hands went to my shoulders as he lowered his head, kissed me. Ravaged me.

I was sinking, drowning, swirling, dizzy. His tongue found mine, mated, sucked, licked. His mouth claimed. Heat surged through me, my mind went blank. I gave myself over to the kiss. To him. To *us.*

His calloused palms slid lower down my arms, then back up, my nerve endings awakening by the simple touch. Goose bumps rose on my skin, yet I wasn't cold. I was burning up.

But when his hand squeezed my arm where I'd been injured, I flinched. Moaned into his kiss. I was used to the pain, lived with it, but I'd forgotten to steel myself to it. I'd forgotten everything, and it had only been a kiss.

Angh pulled back, looked down at me. His breathing

was ragged, his lips red and slick from the kiss. His eyes were like black fire, but filled with concern. He lifted his hands as if I'd burned him. Perhaps I had, for I felt on fire.

"I hurt you," he said.

I shook my head. "I was already hurt."

He closed his eyes, swore. "That is unacceptable."

"I'm fine. Let's get back to the kissing."

His eyes narrowed. "I *will not* touch you if you are hurt," he repeated, this time the words were darker, deeper, as if it were the beast who spoke. "It is your arm?"

I flared my elbow out. "It is my elbow. I injured it last night." I didn't say more. Didn't need to. I doubted he cared in this moment *how* I had been hurt as much as making it better.

"Do you need a ReGen Pod? We will go to the med center at once."

"No. Absolutely not. It can be healed by a wand."

He lifted his head, looked around the bathing room. "Do you have a wand?"

"In the other room."

He stepped back, allowed me to go first, to retrieve it. It seemed strange to be naked, walking about my quarters with him while we weren't actively making out or having sex. But he'd shut me down as if I'd thrown a bucket of ice water on him and refused to touch me. If I wanted sexy times, I had to fix my arm.

I went to the wall unit, retrieved the ReGen wand and turned it on. I waved it over my arm, the blue light quickly easing the ache. It *did* need a ReGen Pod, but Angh didn't need to know that. Not right now. It wasn't broken, and with the wand's help, would ultimately be healed. I wasn't wasting this night with Angh being unconscious in a pod. No way. A wand would appease him and get me what I wanted a lot faster. Him. Inside me. Like *now*.

After he saw where I was injured, he took the wand from me and waved it himself. "Why didn't you take care of this earlier? I do not like the fact that you did not care for yourself."

Shit. I had to either tell a bigger lie or give him the truth.

"Can't you let it go? I'm fine. I'll be fine." Shit. I was blushing now. I could feel the heat creeping into my cheeks. I knew my chest would turn pink, too. Maybe he wouldn't notice.

I put the wand away and looked up at him. His arms were crossed, his brow raised. Hell. He knew I was evading the question.

"Kira, there will be no orgasm for you until you tell me the truth."

Hardball. Sheesh. "Fine. I—" I stuttered. There was no other explanation for it. But admitting the truth was going to sting. "If I'd gone to medical for my elbow they would have placed me in a ReGen pod. And I would have been healed."

"Exactly." He looked confused.

"Everywhere, Angh. *Everywhere*." There, I admitted it. Vaguely, but I told the truth.

"You are hurt other places?" he asked, his eyes were full of concern.

"Not hurt, not like you're thinking. But there are places that ache."

His eyebrows winged up, but he remained silent. Waiting. Obtuse. Why oh why did a woman have to *spell out every freaking detail?* "I'm sore from you. From us. From the other night. I didn't want that to...go away." I dipped my chin, looked at his still hard cock and reached out to wrap my hand around the thick head. He hadn't gone down at all even through all of this talking. "From your cock. My pussy isn't used to...well, you."

He grinned then. Wickedly. And he had a dimple. How had I missed a dimple? God, I was in trouble. If I weren't already naked, that dimple would have had me tossing my panties at him.

"You wanted to remember our night, what I did to you?"

"Yes."

He growled, most likely the growl came from the beast informing me of its pleasure with my words.

He ignored the hand I had around his cock and reached for my elbow, his gigantic hands holding the joint like I was delicate as a hummingbird. "Are you well now?" he asked.

I shifted my arm, moved it to test whether the wand had done its job. It had and it had done it quickly. Perhaps I hadn't been as hurt as I'd thought, that a wand was all I'd needed to begin with. Or maybe I was so high on lust for my beast that my body pretty much didn't care about anything else.

"Yes. And I want you." Only our breathing filled the room now. Concern was gone from his eyes. Need was back.

"Good."

He scooped me up, carried me to my bed and laid me down on my back. He followed me, his hand by my head to hold the bulk of his weight off of me. A thigh slid between mine, parted me and then he shifted so he was settled between my thighs. I felt the thick heat of his cock against my belly.

A hand cupped the back of my knee, lifted it, spread me wide.

"Are you wet for me?"

"Yes," I breathed. The coolness of the bedding at my back was a stark contrast to his heat above me.

He looked at me, studied me.

"I will find out for myself." He kissed my neck, then worked a path down my body, stopping at my breasts to lick and tease my nipples before moving lower. "I will not have you hurt by my cock. You ached from our wild fucking before and you were dripping for me. I will not hurt you if there is a chance you aren't ready."

"I'm ready," I panted.

"I will be the judge of that," he said, his breath fanning over my pussy.

Arching my back, I wanted his mouth, especially since I knew what he could do with it. With his one hand holding my leg up and wide, I was open for him. With his other hand, he circled my entrance with the tip of his blunt finger. "So wet."

"I told you."

"Yes, you are wet. Ready, no."

His finger dipped inside, just the tiniest amount and I bucked. His hands were like dinner plates, his finger smaller than a cock but still quite large. He was teasing me and I rippled around him, trying to pull him deeper. But there was no moving the beast. Instead, he moved in decadent little circles just inside my entrance as his tongue moved in the same leisurely fashion over my clit.

"Angh!" I cried, my hands going to his head, tangling in his hair.

I was primed. I'd been primed for an orgasm since the second I saw him in the fighting pit. Nothing had changed since then. I'd come from his skill so many times that one night and I should have been satisfied. No, it had only made me eager for more. So foreplay wasn't needed to get me all revved up. In fact, I arched my back and cried out my pleasure, my first orgasm of the night just by the most basic—yet intimate—of contact.

"God, oh. My. God." I practically ripped his hair out as I came. He didn't speed up his pace, didn't relent on the teasing motion of his finger, the flick of his tongue.

"Angh!" I cried toward the ceiling, but he wouldn't stop.

I came again, my body lost to him. I was at his mercy, the heat, the need, the bliss.

Finally, after minutes, hours, days, he lifted his head, slipped his finger from me.

"You're wet. You're ready," he said, using the back of his hand to wipe his glistening mouth.

I couldn't talk, couldn't tell the stupid beast I'd been ready all along, but he was an alpha Atlan, all dominant and orally skilled. Damn him.

He didn't delay now, only levered himself back over me, pushing my knee up and back so he could settle his hips against mine, his cock at my entrance.

"Now," I breathed.

He slid deep, stretching me wide. My inner walls rippled and stretched to take all of him. Since his finger hadn't gone deep, I groaned at finally having something inside me. And that something felt like soft velvet over steel. Huge, long, thick, hot.

It filled me and filled me and filled me some more. Only when his hips pressed against mine did I know I'd taken all of him.

I blinked, opened my eyes to see Angh gazing at me. His eyes were almost black, his jaw clenched tight. Sweat dotted his brow and he was holding back. Panting. Straining.

"Angh, please," I begged.

"I will not hurt you."

I shook my head, my hair sliding across the bedding. "You won't. Fuck me. Fuck me hard like you want. Like we both need."

He pulled back, thrust deep. Hard. Again.

"Yes!" I cried, assuring him I wanted it. Needed it as much as he did.

His hand on my leg tightened, the grip strong as he fucked me with abandon. Hard and deep lunges of his hips, his cock sliding and rubbing over every pleasure spot in me. The head of his cock bumped the end of my passage. He rubbed against my clit and since it was so sensitive, so primed for more orgasms, I didn't need to touch myself, didn't need him to do it either. I came as he took me, the feel of him deep, so deep, set me off. I screamed, thrashed, grabbed his back, clawed it. Gave over to it. Perhaps I had a little bit of a beast within me as well.

Angh thrust deep one last time, his muscles going taut as he held himself still. He groaned, then growled as he came, emptying himself in me. All of him. I felt the hot wash of his seed as it coated me, filled me to overflowing.

We were hot and sweaty, a sticky mess. It was perfect.

Angh didn't take time to catch his breath, but angled his body so we rolled. He was on his back and I was straddling him, his cock still deep in me. Still hard as if he hadn't just come. His hands went to my hips and he lifted me up, lowered me back down.

My eyes flared at the feel of this new angle. I was so wet from him, the slide easy. His seed coated us, made me slippery as I wiggled on him.

"Again," he said, looking up at me. His hands moved to my breasts, cupped them, played with them. "Fuck me, mate. Use my cock for your pleasure. My beast and I want to watch."

I couldn't deny him. Why should I? I had a beast cock deep in my pussy, three orgasms already on my scorecard and he wanted me to have more.

I began to move, to use him for my pleasure. I couldn't get enough.

But one night would have to be it. It would have to do. So I put my hands on his broad chest and fucked him. Gave over to it. To him. Gave him and the beast exactly what they wanted.

When we were finally both spent, I napped, lying on top of his chest, his cock still inside me. Neither of us seemed to want a moment of separation. He pulled the blankets over us and I was drifting, loving him, listening to the beat of his heart as he stroked my body like he couldn't stop touching me. God, I was so in love with him, it hurt.

This was nuts. I *was* nuts. On Earth, there were dates. Dinner and a movie. Walks in the park. A getting-to-know-you period. Rules about not sleeping with a guy on the first date. There were even various relationship statuses. Going out, hooking up, exclusive, friends with benefits, no strings sex all put a couple in a certain *place.* But with Angh, it had been...*bam.* Just a glance at each other across the fighting pit and that had been it. I'd wanted him. He'd wanted me. Done.

He'd known I was his mate then and there. Perhaps I had known the same as well, but I'd been tricking myself into thinking otherwise.

There was nothing I could do to stop the tears. They burned my eyes and no amount of blinking stopped the build-up of pain that dripped from me, agony sliding onto his chest one salty tear at a time. It shouldn't hurt like this. A fling should be easy. A quick, hard fuck to scratch the itch and move on.

His hands covered my entire back, stroking me gently. "Did I hurt you, Kira?" His voice was a low rumble and I laughed, the sound more pain than humor.

"No, Angh. You're perfect. I just don't want this night to end."

He stopped breathing, his heart suddenly pounding beneath my ear as he sat up. With a groan, he slipped his cock from my swollen core and shifted us both so that I sat on his lap. His huge shoulders blocked out half of the wall panel above my bed and I stared, trying to burn the image into my mind so I could take it out later and savor it.

Remember that he was real and not a dream. Remember the look in his eyes as he stared at me as if I were the most precious thing in the universe. The way his whiskers were coming in quickly. How warm and solid he felt beneath me. How gentle his hands were in comparison to how ruthless he was on the battlefield.

And suddenly, one more night with him seemed like the biggest fucking mistake I'd ever made in my life. How was I supposed to walk away? I loved him. It was the truth. He was everything I'd ever wanted in a mate. Strong. Honorable. Caring. Dominant. A sexual maniac and absolutely loyal. Having to walk away from *this* was going to feel like ripping my still beating heart right out of my chest and stomping on it with combat boots.

He leaned over slightly and it was then I saw the second set of cuffs, the smaller set, *my* set partially hidden beneath the stack of clothing he'd placed on the small table next to the bed. He pulled them free and settled them on my lap.

Shaking, I wrapped my fingers around the cool metal. I'd never wanted anything more than I wanted to walk into the Vice Admiral's office, hold up my wrists so she could see the cuffs there and tell her to stick my next mission where the sun didn't shine.

But that would mean people were going to die. Who and how many? I had no idea. But Commander Phan and I were making progress. Our last trip out there to take down the mines, I'd heard the buzzing. It was more than I'd heard before. And there were more minefields hidden in space. Dozens of them. More deploying every day, beating us. *Killing* us.

What was my happiness when an entire battlegroup was depending on me to keep them alive? Thousands of warriors, their mates and their children?

I couldn't be selfish. I wasn't raised that way. Protect and serve. That's what I did. Nowhere in the job description did that include falling in love with an Atlan and going off to live on what amounted to a glorified prison colony. I'd have great sex, make wonderful babies, and spend the rest of my life wondering what my happiness was costing the rest of the Coalition.

And then there was Angh. My Angh. But he was Warlord Anghar, a legendary warrior and soon-to-be recruit of the Intelligence Core himself.

Our mating wouldn't just cost the I.C. one Hive Communications specialist, but two.

"I want you to be my mate, Kira." His huge hand tunneled under my hair and gently turned my tear-streaked face up to look at him. His thumb swiped the wetness away. "I will give you everything. Everything I am and everything I have is yours."

I couldn't do it, couldn't look him in the eye and say what I had to say. So I leaned forward and kissed his chest before resting my cheek there. His chin settled on top of my hair and I caressed the dark swirling designs in the cuffs as I confessed.

"I want to, Angh. But I can't. I'm not what you think I am."

"And what is that? You are mine, Kira. I can feel it. My beast knows that he is yours. The way you give yourself to me, I know you feel it, too."

Tears. More tears. His voice was so gentle, so deep and honest. I wasn't supposed to tell him anything, but I couldn't hurt him and not tell him why. I might have to walk away, but he'd know the truth first. "I'm not an instructor at the Academy. Well, I am, but that's not *all* I am."

When he remained silent, I took a deep breath, fought

off the shuddering of my diaphragm that made my voice wobble, and forced the words out. "I am a top level I.C. operative. I can't tell you what I do, or who I report to, but I have two more years on my contract and they own me, Angh. Own everything I do, including deciding if I can take a mate. I can't get out of it and I'm not sure walking away would be the right thing to do."

His hand ran down my side to my elbow and his fingertips traced over my now forgotten injury. For me, it was nothing. Over. For him, it was something else and I felt him putting the clues together like a master strategist snapping the final pieces of a puzzle into place. "A Hive Soldier gave you that bruise."

"Yes."

"How?"

"I can't tell you that."

He sighed. "I knew when I saw you in the battle simulation that you were more than you seemed, mate."

"I'm not your mate, Angh."

"You are mine, Kira. Whether you wear the cuffs or not, my beast and I know who we belong to."

I smacked him on the shoulder, although it did nothing to him and made my palm sting. "Damn it, Angh! Yell at me or something. This sucks. It's not fair. You want to be with me and I want to be with you. And this stupid war is going to ruin everything."

There was no reaction from him this time, he was solid and warm, an immovable object. "War is never easy. And we are warriors, not innocent children. We know the cost." He lowered his hand to my lap and pulled the smaller cuffs from my hands, dropping them onto the floor next to the bed, out of sight, as if they were inconsequential. Nothing. "I know you cannot tell me much, but I must know, if you walk away from the I.C., will warriors die?"

I sighed. "Yes."

"How many?"

"Thousands. Maybe more." If we didn't bring down the minefields, and the battlegroups were pushed back or destroyed, entire worlds could fall.

He moved again, lying down in the bed and pulling me into his arms. My tears were gone, but the salty taste lingered when I licked my lips. "I'm sorry, Angh. I don't know what to do."

"I do." He wrapped his arms around me and pressed me to his chest, held me close. "You will rest, mate, and in the morning, I will return to The Colony and you will do what needs to be done to save lives and win this war. I admire you, Kira. I knew my mate would be fierce. Strong. But you are honorable as well. You are a warrior in heart and mind and I cannot sacrifice thousands of lives for our personal happiness. You are right, my one true mate. As much as it hurts both of us, *you are right*. We cannot be together."

I sobbed and he held me. It was painful, and beautiful, and it broke me in so many ways I wasn't sure I'd ever recover.

When the comms unit attached to his armor that had been tossed to the floor buzzed a few minutes later and Vice Admiral Niobe *requested* Angh's presence in her office first thing in the morning, I knew we had both made the right choice. We couldn't be together, but Angh was wrong about one thing. He wasn't going back to The Colony. He was going out there to fight, just like I was.

Commander Phan needed him to help her defend Battlegroup Karter, not me. They were a powerful unit that could *hear* the Hive and that skill, their powerful combination, couldn't be ignored.

I already had my next assignment, a recon mission to extract a top I.C. weapons specialist from a Hive Integration Unit on one of the outlying sectors. I had to leave in a few hours, about the time Angh believed he would be transporting back to The Colony.

A few more hours and then I had no idea if I would ever see the warrior I loved again.

I didn't sleep. Neither did he. We held each other. Touched, breathed, kissed, stroked. We made love, slowly. It was tender and precious and good-bye.

10

ngh, Vice Admiral Niobe's office, Coalition Academy, Zioria

"COME IN, WARLORD," THE VICE ADMIRAL SAID, RISING from the chair behind her desk. Her office was in a prime location. On the first floor of the administration building —on the far side of the campus from where Kira's classroom was—she was afforded views of the central quad from windows on two sides.

From my quick assessment of the female, the Academy head was my age. She wore the uniform of the Coalition Academy, the dark black color signifying her role as an instructor, but the epaulets on her shoulders indicated her superior status. Her manner was crisp, her chin tilted up in a way that indicated this wasn't a social call.

Fine with me. I was in no mood to talk. I was in no mood for anything but having Kira back in my arms. But that was not to be.

I took a deep breath as I stepped into the tidy office, trying to keep my beast under control. Ever since Kira had told me the truth, it had raged, howling in frustration and agony. The cuffs about my wrists were the only things keeping the animal within in check. My beast should have been eased by the fact that I'd just spilled my seed deep inside Kira's pussy, again, but facing the truth was like jumping in a freezing Atlan lake. Any sexual satisfaction I'd felt was gone. Especially standing here. I wanted Kira. I had no desire to be summoned by the Vice Admiral. While attractive enough, she wasn't the female I wanted to fuck. To mate. To *claim.*

I assumed she was adding me to the next scheduled transport slot for The Colony, although she could have just directed me to the transport center instead of her office. I had destroyed Academy property, fucked an instructor and probably broken ten other Academy rules. It wasn't as if I'd been subtle in my behavior, and as leader, she'd have to set an example of me, or at least get me the fuck off Zioria.

I didn't care. It didn't matter what she did to me now. Kira and I couldn't be together. Nothing else mattered. My beast growled and I closed my eyes, breathed through my nose to keep from going into beast mode. The heat, the craze of the fever was building. I knew it. I felt it. My beast was succumbing to it with Kira's situation, the desolate future we faced without her. There was no reason for me or my beast to keep fighting, to hold the fever back any longer.

The Vice Admiral's eyes narrowed as she watched me try to gain control. I sighed. The pain I'd endured at the hands of the Hive was nothing in comparison to the ache

I felt now. Losing Kira was the worst torture imaginable. Death was something I now welcomed. It was now the only thing that could bring me the peace I so desperately desired. I'd stolen moments of it with Kira in my arms, but she wasn't meant to be mine. I had offered her everything I had, heart, body and soul, and fate was against us.

This war was against us.

The Hive had taken everything from me after all.

I hadn't thought I could survive the Hive Integration Unit, or the endless agony of their *modifications* as they forced me to become one of them. Then I had faced the desolation and loneliness of life on The Colony. I'd survived all of it. But this? I wasn't wrong, hadn't been wrong even when I'd told Seth, my friend on a ReCon team who had refused to put me out of my misery. Instead, he'd saved me. I had no idea why, now. I was better off dead than without my mate. And leaving her? The ion blast that would ultimately kill me would hurt less.

"I am unstable," I said simply. "I am prepared to die."

One dark brow cocked upward, but otherwise she offered no emotion. "I would tell you to sit, Warlord, but I doubt it would be comfortable for you in your current state."

No, being forced into a chair while my beast prowled and all but howled in agony would be impossible.

"I am glad you are prepared to die, as all fighters going into battle must come to terms with that reality," she continued. "In the Intelligence Core, the chances of survival are even lower than on standard battle ops."

I remained silent, hoping she'd get to her point

quickly enough. I knew everything she said was the truth, but I was no new recruit. I was old. Not in body—I was an Atlan in my prime—but my soul? I felt like I'd been alive too long already, been through too much. The burden was heavy. For Kira, I could face it. But alone? Alone, the beast would rise to the surface and force my hand. I would become a danger to everyone I encountered. A truly merciless beast with no thought but destruction.

I could not allow that to happen. I'd fought too long, too hard to be honorable. To hold true to the teachings of my father and grandfather. They were long dead, but they lived on in me, in the strength of my will and the determination I had to survive. I was not weak, but I was tired. A walking time-bomb. I had neither the time nor patience for games. "Why am I here, Vice Admiral?"

She leaned back in her chair, her pointer finger tapping slowly on the top of her desk as she held my gaze. "I met a colleague of yours the other day. A friend, from what I've been told. Commander Chloe Phan."

It was my turn to raise a brow. "Yes. I am familiar with the commander." I wasn't going to say anything more about my friend, or her mates, until I knew where this was going.

"I heard a rumor that the two of you brought one of the webs down together. The very first mine attack, on Battlegroup Karter. I was told you were there." She watched me for a reaction. Silence filled the room and I refused to confirm or deny anything. What was she doing? Had Chloe somehow gotten into trouble? "Well? Are the rumors true?" Silent, she stood in front of me and waited, the desk the only object between us.

"I don't know what you're talking about," I said through gritted teeth.

She gave a slight nod of her head. Her dark hair was pulled back severely, parted down the center and tucked into a bun at the nape of her neck. "Good, you're able to keep secrets."

"Vice Admiral—" I began, but she lifted her hand to cut me off.

"Your classified work with Commander Phan is the only reference needed for what I have planned. I need you to come work for me."

The corner of my mouth tipped up. It would normally be a small smile, but now, it was all sneer. "I doubt the doors here at the Academy would survive my employment as an instructor."

"Yes, that is true. However, your role will not be here, at the Academy, but with the I.C. And this will not be a one-time mission, like you experienced with Commander Phan, but in a full-time capacity. I need someone with your skills, with your expertise." She pointed to my head and I knew she referred to the implant the doctors on The Colony had been unable to remove, the Hive technology imbedded so deeply inside my brain tissue that removing it would have killed me.

I crossed my arms over my chest. I stood over a foot taller than the female and was easily twice her weight. She did not seem concerned I might hurt her or that my beast might rage and snap her like a twig. "You work for the I.C.?" Gods curse the I.C. and these females. First, I lose the only female I've ever loved, and now this one wanted me to be her puppet.

She nodded once, succinctly. "That is correct. Your

ability to *hear* the Hive is crucial to moving our battlegroups forward. As you're well aware, the removal of the network of mines that initially attacked Battlegroup Karter was a success, but the Karter is stalled. Blocked by a new Hive deployment. They updated their systems after their mines were destroyed in that sector and we have not been able to duplicate your success. The Hive continues to deploy new minefields like spiders spinning their webs. They are surrounding us, Warlord. I need you to work with Commander Phan to bring the other Hive minefields down. You'll start with the Karter and go from there."

"It's going to be pretty hard to fight the Hive if I'm dead."

"We will do everything in our power to keep you alive. The I.C. has fighter groups, squadrons of Prillon flyers, even other Atlans at our disposal if we need them."

I shook my head slowly. "I won't make it that long." I held up my cuffs so they were between us. She couldn't miss them. "I might survive one of your missions, two if we're both lucky, but I've got Mating Fever."

She swore under her breath. It was the first time I'd seen any kind of emotion from her. Being an Everian Hunter, I expected her to be a little less...pent up, their Hunters infamously calm under pressure. She fit that, but she was also passionate about her job. A requirement in her two roles as Academy leader and I.C. Vice Admiral, but not normal for the females I grew up with, the serene and compassionate females on Atlan.

Staring at her, I wondered why she had yet to mate, to find a worthy Hunter from her home planet to take care of her in a way only he could. Wondered if the mark on her palm had ever flared to life, made her go crazy to find the one person who was her perfect match. To be with the one male in the universe, in a custom to which she was familiar. I could only surmise a night with her mate would make her far less...prickly.

"I assume, based on the fact that you came to Zioria and ripped the door off of Instructor Dahl's classroom, that she is your mate."

"She is."

"Very well. I will pull her from active duty at once."

"No." The one word sounded like an ion cannon in the small room. Kira was an honorable warrior. She would not want to live with the fact that she was being forced to sit on the sidelines when she was clearly needed.

"Get those cuffs on her, and I don't much care how you do it," the Vice Admiral commanded, as if it were as simple as clicking the cuffs closed.

"She works for you," I replied, as if that explained everything.

The Vice Admiral's brow arched and she was less than pleased at discovering Kira had shared secrets. "So, she is also a confidentiality risk."

"No."

"Then how do you know she works for me?"

"Look, I'm not in the mood for this and neither is my beast. Captain Dahl is an honorable warrior. I want the cuffs on her. Do you think I want to succumb to the fever when I can have her?" I sighed, but it did nothing to calm me. "She confessed to me that we couldn't be together because she works for the I.C. She didn't name names or tell me what she does, but I am not a cadet. I know what's out there. You know what I've done. I've seen better warriors than you die. I've survived the Hive, fought in so many battles I lost count. Do not insult my intelligence. And do not insult me or my mate again."

The idea did not sit well with my beast. In fact, the thought of Kira being insulted or maligned in any way made my beast furious. She'd lain in my arms last night, completely broken, and for what? This woman and her lack of respect? I would not allow that.

"You will die if you don't get those cuffs on her," she countered. "You'll be executed. I spoke to Governor Rone about you, and Lieutenant Denzel. I know why he was ordered to accompany you, Warlord. And I am not amused."

"Yes, I will. I *will* die before I force her to be my mate. She made her choice. It is her decision and *only* hers." I touched the other cuffs affixed to my belt, the small set that should have been about her wrists. "She refused my cuffs. She refused me."

"That is understandable." The Vice Admiral sat back down, her arms crossed over her chest and she did not look any happier than I felt. "She is an instructor here, yes. But she *works* for me. For the I.C. She is an indispensable asset to the team. You may have decided she is your mate, but she's not free to make such a choice. She belongs to the Coalition. There are not enough I.C. assets with Hive communication implants to go around. I can't afford to keep you two together. Unless the implants in both of your heads have somehow magically connected?" Her voice was not hopeful, but curious. "Heard any strange buzzing when you're together? Like the implants in your head and hers are trying to communicate?"

What the fuck was this woman talking about? I lifted a

hand to my neck and traced the thick outline of the scar there with my fingertips. Kira did have a scar on her neck, but it was off to the side, closer to her ear.

Just like Commander Phan's.

But even if my mate did have the implant, there was no connection between the two of us that I was aware of —other than being mates. I would not lie, not about this. Too many lives were at stake.

"No. I'm sorry, but there was nothing. I didn't know Kira had an implant similar to mine."

"That's what I thought." She leaned forward and used her fingers to manipulate the digital files just visible on her desktop workstation. "I will pull her from field ops effective immediately."

"No."

"Look, Warlord, she tried to work with Commander Phan and failed. Right now, I'm staring down the potential loss of Battlegroup Karter and all of Sector 437. There are several planets in that sector that the Hive will overrun in a matter of months if we can't maintain Coalition control. I need you more than I need her, and I need you alive. She's out. You're in. I'll throw her in the damn brig if I have to, to force your cooperation. It's not up for debate."

"Are you threatening Kira?" My voice was low, too low. I was riding the razor's edge of control.

The Vice Admiral didn't bother to look up at me, as if my compliance were guaranteed. The threat I posed one not worthy of her attention. She was a fool. She had just threatened my mate. Atlans had killed for less and they hadn't been in Mating Fever.

She moved her fingers over the screen and I saw an

image of Kira in a cadet's uniform. She looked so much younger, innocent. Her eyes in the photo were sparkling with excitement and hope. Not the devastated look I'd seen in them last night, heard in her voice, felt in her every touch as we'd fucked one final time.

"I don't think you understand, Warlord. Kira is mine. I own her. By Coalition law, the only way out of her contract with the I.C. is to die or be injured so severely she is unable to continue."

"She has a mate. If she accepts my cuffs, she will be free of you. I'll go direct to Commander Karter myself." He owed me, that Prillon bastard. I'd saved his entire Battlegroup with Chloe. If I needed something, he'd come through. He'd go to Prime Nial if he had to. I'd see to that.

"Makes no difference. She's human. They don't have the same…issues the rest of you do. As an Everian, I understand. But there is no relief clause in a human's contract for mating."

I thought of Denzel, of the way he watched Melody, the way his eyes never left her and his entire being focused on her wellbeing. I wanted to see this cold-hearted bitch say that to Denzel and watch the monster she would unleash. "You will leave Kira out of this."

"I won't. She's your mate. I need you alive. If she's not willing to cooperate, I will force her compliance. A few years in confinement won't hurt her. You'll be granted conjugal visits. The faster you get the Hive threat taken care of, the sooner your mate will be free." She glanced up from the desk, her gaze like ice. The female thought she'd won, that I would do what she commanded simply because she threatened my mate. She was wrong, but she kept talking. "After that, you can go to Atlan or The

Colony or wherever you want to and start making little Atlan babies. That will be all. Don't try to leave the planet. I've placed a transport block on both you and Captain Dahl. You're dismissed."

My beast went deadly still. This female had threatened my mate. Threatened to *use me* as a means of *hurting* Kira. Conjugal fucking visits? Transport block? *Years* in confinement?

The beast took control in the space between one heartbeat and the next and I transformed. My shoulders thickened. The bones in my face shifted as the monster she'd roused burst from me with a roar of rage that rattled the lights.

I gave in to the rage, tearing the mating cuffs off my wrists and dropping them, forgotten, at my feet. Nothing could hold back the fever now.

No one was going to use what was between me and Kira to control her, to manipulate her or me. To *use* us against one another.

I'd tear this fucking planet apart piece by fucking piece before that happened.

I lifted the desk from the floor and threw it at the wall so hard it imbedded in the rough surface. The Vice Admiral had the sense to look scared. My beast wanted to kill her, rip her arms and legs off her body like a tortured insect before finishing her.

She'd threatened our mate.

The doors opened and I took several hits of blaster fire before falling to my knees. This was what I'd wanted. The beast wanted to hurt the one who'd threatened us, but I was smarter than that. I knew we couldn't do what the Vice Admiral wanted us to do. I would not condemn Kira to years in prison so this bitch could play with me like a toy, sending me out on pet projects and rewarding me with my mate's pussy when she felt I'd earned it.

I'd rather die. And the beast agreed.

The blasts increased in intensity. I smelled the burning of my own flesh and smiled, the beast meeting the Vice Admiral's gaze with a giant grin.

"Fuck. You." He spoke for both of us.

The Vice Admiral screamed that she wanted me alive, but I was still grinning when everything went black.

11

"HE'S BIG, KIRA. EVERYWHERE. AND THE THINGS THAT MAN can do with his tongue. I thought I was going to die."

"I'm happy for you. I am." Melody sat across from me in our usual spot in the Academy cafeteria. The room was mostly empty, the crew cleaning up at the tail end of the breakfast service. I needed to be someplace public so I wouldn't start to cry again. I knew Melody would be here before her morning classes and practical assessments, and I'd been right. We weren't alone, but there wasn't anyone sitting near us to overhear her oversharing.

She leaned over the table to get closer to me, the front of her uniform in jeopardy of getting in her plate of breakfast. The food was mostly gone, but she'd have to return to her quarters and change if her uniform were stained. Yes, this was what I was considering as I listened to my friend talk about Denzel as if he were a piece of man candy.

To her, he was.

I was happy for her. Thrilled. I knew how it felt to find The One. I recognized her excitement, her sheer joy. I'd felt it in myself. But she wasn't facing the blinding heartache, the pain of walking away from The One. No, she could have Denzel if she wanted. As a cadet, and one from Earth, she was a volunteer and could quit at any time. She hadn't signed her life away. Being a standard fighter was not the same as committing to the Intelligence Core. Once she was mated, she'd be free. And choosing a mate from The Colony would allow her to remain in space. If she desired, she didn't have to go back to Earth, instead joining Denzel on The Colony. Since mates were few and far between, they wanted all the females they could get. Women warriors were a small percentage of the fighting force to begin with, as the Prillons, Atlans and several other races didn't allow their women to join the fight. When a female from one of the other races wanted to walk away, they practically shoved her out of the Fleet with bells and ribbons.

They valued their mates above all. Family. Life. They were all out here protecting life and didn't understand why any race would allow their women to fight. Which just made most of us more determined to prove our worth. To be brilliant and merciless.

Walking away had become a mark of weakness in my mind, not strength. And it had cost me everything. Cost me Angh.

I pushed down the pain, shoved it in a box and sat on the mental lid as I listened to her. I couldn't smile; it was impossible. But I could be happy for her, listen to her prattle on about how fabulous Denzel was. I didn't blame her this. She was cute about it, and it was sweet to see her so in love. So happy.

"I *was* going to quit." Those words cut through my thoughts. "Leave with Denzel on the transport later today."

"What?" I'd heard her, at least that she was quitting. I'd blurred out the mention of his skill in bed and anything else since she mentioned his size. I had no doubt he was more than adequate in that department, but he was no beast. "No. Mel. You can't quit."

She gave a shrug that was so casual, completely at odds with her intentions. Quitting the Academy was a big deal. A few were kicked out. A few found their mate, like the Everians, and had to leave. But it was rare for someone to outright quit and walk away. Especially as far along in training as Melody was.

"I *was*. But I have two weeks to go until graduation and while I love Denzel and want to be with him, I'm not going to give up finishing for him."

Good. She wasn't stupid. On Earth, I'd heard of so many women giving up their lives, their goals and dreams for a man. Then, when the guy dumped her, she was left with nothing. I refused to let Melody give up the status of an officer trained in the Coalition Academy when she'd come so far, sacrificed blood, sweat and tears. Graduation was so close.

"I need to know that I did it. While I might live on The Colony as Denzel's mate, I need to be valuable. Being an officer will ensure I can be included. Useful." She grinned slyly. "Useful for more than jumping Denzel every chance I get."

I exhaled, smiled at her. Relieved. "God, I thought for a second there I was going to have to take you out to the firing range and put you as a target." It was my turn to lean in. "Never be beholden to a man. Give yourself a way out. I want things to work out for you with Denzel. You have no idea how much." I put my hand on her wrist, reminding me that I hadn't put on Angh's cuffs. *Shit.* I swallowed, continued. "But if for some reason it doesn't, then you can get an assignment that gets you off The Colony. Or, you can take assignments *and* be his mate."

She laughed at that. "You think he'll let me go fight the Hive?"

I shrugged. "If he wants to be your mate, he has to let you live your dreams."

Her smile slipped and she studied me. "Shouldn't I be saying the exact same thing to you? What about you? Will Angh let you live your dreams?"

My dreams. *My dreams.* It was completely and totally opposite of everything I'd just said to Melody. I wanted to quit and live a quiet life on The Colony with Angh. He'd been through so much, so much more than any one male could take. He deserved peace. A mate. Children. Happiness. And I wanted to be a part of that.

I was so tired of fighting, of my life in the I.C., being an instructor. I'd given so much I wanted…well, what I *wanted.* And that was Angh.

I wanted Angh.

I thought of Melody and if she quit the Academy. There was always another cadet ready to take her spot. She was replaceable. *I* was replaceable. If I left the I.C.—

even by breaking the law—someone else would take my spot. People might die, but not because I personally quit. People would die because of the Hive. Dr. Helion probably had more fighters with the implants in their brain. I wasn't the only one. I wasn't crucial. But I was crucial to Angh and he was *crucial* to me.

"Don't laugh," I said.

She cocked her head to the side, studied me. "All right." She knew I was serious, that whatever I was going to say was important. I never shared my feelings. Hell, it had taken tons of prodding to get me to have that one-night-stand with Angh after the fighting pits. And look where that got me.

"And don't tell me to take my words and shove it."

She nodded once.

"I'm quitting. Walking away." I looked at the comm unit on my wrist and realized I'd made the decision before meeting her for breakfast. I was never late for an op. Never. "I was supposed to be at the transport center ten minutes ago."

Melody's eyes widened, but she said nothing.

I laughed, but it was dry and without humor. I ran my hand over my head. "I'm in love with Angh and I want to be with him."

She did smile then, a slow, soft one. Her eyes held... pity? "You aren't wearing his cuffs."

I swallowed a lump in my throat. I wouldn't cry. Not here, not now. Nope.

"I refused them."

"Why? You love him, that's obvious. And he ripped a door off your classroom. I'd say it's obvious to everyone on Zioria what he feels for you."

I shook my head. "I can't talk about it. I was going to let him go, but I've changed my mind. The transport window for The Colony opens up in a couple of hours. I'm sure he'll be on it. I want to be with him." I ached to find Angh and drag him to transport, hold my ion pistol to the transport technician's head and force a transport if I had to. Now that I'd made up my mind, I wanted Angh.

Now.

"I'm leaving on the next transport window. I don't care what happens."

"If you didn't show up to go do something I'm not supposed to know about, you're AWOL now," Melody reminded me. "They're not going to clear you to transport anywhere. The Vice Admiral will throw you in the brig, or they'll send you home."

Yeah, she knew I was more than an instructor, but hadn't said anything. I often disappeared from Zioria, had substitutes teach my class without me saying a word about it to her. She was my BFF here and I kept her clueless. Thankfully, she knew I did *something*, but she wasn't sure what.

"I have to take the risk. I'll call in favors. I have friends everywhere. Lots of them." I could work from The Colony. There was no reason I couldn't transport from The Colony for my missions. It would just take a bit of extra planning. If the Vice Admiral wanted me so bad, she could have me. On my terms.

Denzel walked up, stood behind Melody and put his hand on her shoulder. We both looked up at him.

"What's the matter?" Melody asked. He looked grim, but while he had an easy smile, the man often looked that way. Perhaps that was a side effect of being captured by the Hive. Whatever it was, he still wasn't as grim as Angh.

Denzel dropped something onto the table in front of me, the metal clanging as it hit the hard, polished surface.

I gasped.

Cuffs. Mating cuffs. I'd recognize these anywhere. But they weren't just mine. There were four of them.

I glanced up at Denzel.

"He's in the brig."

My eyes widened and my mouth fell open. "What? Why? I thought you were both transporting back to The Colony?"

Denzel shook my head. "I came here with Angh to get you. My job was to keep him in check, to keep his beast in check. If he didn't return with you, it's my job to execute him."

I stood abruptly, my chair scraping across the floor before tipping over. "What?"

"He's in Mating Fever. Has been since the fighting pit. Since the first time he was with you."

Mating Fever. Shit. Shit. Shit.

"He doesn't have to *die.*"

"He does. The only way the fever can be broken is by a claiming. Claiming his mate."

Me.

"But—"

Denzel lifted a hand, cut me off. "It's too late for that now. He attacked the Vice Admiral. He ripped off his cuffs. Nothing is controlling his beast now. A delegation from Atlan is coming for him. He's not fighting it. He's prepared to die."

131

Melody stood too, wrapped her arms around Denzel. "They won't ask you to kill your friend, will they?"

"No, but I will. It is the honorable thing to do," he murmured, then kissed the top of her head. "He trusted me to see it done. I won't break that trust. Not in this."

She looked up into his eyes and they stood like that, frozen in time. I saw the bond between them. There was no inner beast, no mark, no mating collars. They were both human. Yet they were mates. There was no question. The silly heat in Melody's eyes when I'd first sat down was gone. I only saw love now. Bonding. Shared pain.

Connection.

I had that with Angh, but had walked away from it because of duty. Honor.

Honor?

What honor was there in my job if I didn't have Angh to come back to? Who was I fighting for? *What* was I fighting for if not the connection, the love people shared? I had it and I'd tossed it aside, just as Denzel had tossed the cuffs on the table.

"Fuck this," I said to myself, staring at Denzel but not seeing him. "Fuck this!" I repeated, this time louder. A few heads turned my way, but I didn't care.

Angh was in trouble. I was already AWOL, already committed to him. He wasn't going back to The Colony. He was here. In the brig. Ready to die.

"The Vice Admiral can just fucking deal. She can have me, but she gets my beast, too."

I grabbed the cuffs and stormed out of the cafeteria. It was time to claim my mate.

12

THE VICE ADMIRAL'S DOOR WAS CLOSED. I COULD SEE THAT it was down the long hallway and walked straight there as her assistant chased me, mumbling bullshit about Niobe being on a *very important call.*

Whatever. I'd show her a fucking important call. Angh was in the brig? Scheduled for execution?

No. Heads were going to roll and it wasn't going to be my mate's. The Vice Admiral's, if necessary.

When the door wouldn't open, I cursed a human blue streak, then used my emergency code to override the lock. Rank had its privileges.

"Captain," the assistant called. "What do you think you are doing? You can't go in there!"

I turned, my hand on the ion blaster at my hip. I didn't draw the weapon, but the threat was there. It was real, very fucking real. "Get out of here," I practically snarled. I definitely had a little beast in me. "This doesn't concern you."

The Prillon cadet who had scurried after me took one look into my eyes and backed up with her hands in the air. "All right." She turned on her heel and stormed back to her desk. "But I'm calling security. *Again.* I don't get paid enough for this damn job."

Now that the lock was disabled, one wave of my palm and the door slid open to reveal...chaos.

The Vice Admiral's desk was imbedded in the wall, fully one third of it no longer visible as the remaining two legs dangled in the air. The other two had been ripped from the bottom of the desk and scattered in a random pattern on the floor. There were burns from ion blaster fire all over the walls behind the desk and I could just imagine a couple of asshole security guards standing where I stood now, in the doorway, firing at my mate.

Yes. My mate.

He was mine. I was over the bureaucratic bullshit. And seeing the scorch marks proved the powers that be considered the rules more important than anything else. I could only imagine what had set Angh's beast off to destroy the room—and to require so much fire power to stun him and bring him into control.

And those stupid-ass rules? Angh and I would figure it out for ourselves. If we had to be apart for a few weeks at a time, we'd just have to deal. I wasn't letting him go. Not unless he didn't want me anymore. And judging by the sore, still swollen state of my pussy and the whisker burns all over my body, *that* was not going to be an issue.

My fingers wrapped around the hilt of my blaster as I

surveyed the rest of the damage. Overturned chairs. Blood on the floor. God help this bitch if it was Angh's.

Speaking of...

The Vice Admiral stood in the corner away from the mess, sipping from a small glass, staring out over the grounds through one of her many windows. From the look and smell of it, the liquid in her glass was strong, but clear. Not whiskey, but definitely alcoholic, and I had to wonder if it were her first. Two of the windows were shattered, the web pattern an indication that something rather large, like a Prillon guard, had been thrown into it. The glass—or whatever it was made of—was bulletproof, I knew that much. So whatever had hit them had been big and hard, and held a lot of force.

Good. Hopefully Angh gave as good as he got.

"Is the blood his, Niobe?" I refused to address her in any way other than woman to woman. We'd been on dozens of missions together, saved each other's lives. I had thought, at the bare minimum, we respected each other. This shit was personal, and she knew it. What she'd done, what had happened here, went far beyond the usual BFF problems.

She took another drink and looked over her shoulder at the bloodstains I had indicated. Her snort of laughter contained no humor. "Gods, no. That Atlan is magnificent, isn't he? Sent six guards to medical, and that was after they shot him with tranquilizers. Shame to lose him."

I frowned.

"Lose him? Start talking, Niobe. What the hell happened here? Why is he in the brig? What did you *do*? He was fine a couple of hours ago."

"In your bed, you mean." Her dark brow arched up and I refused to look away from the challenge in her eyes. It wasn't as if she didn't know. Angh had ripped the door off my classroom. Obviously, what we meant to each other was more than just...dating.

"Yes. In my bed. He's mine." I stepped inside the room and closed the distance between us, until we stood facing one another, the broken window at our side. She was close enough to punch in the face, but I knew just how far I could push her without ending up in the brig myself, so I soothed the beast that seemed to live inside me now by stroking the hilt of my blaster. The slight scent coming from her glass smelled like vodka, a distinctly human drink. How she'd become accustomed to something so remote from Everis was beyond me.

The silence stretched, and she turned away from me to once again stare out over the grounds. Down below, dozens of cadets moved from building to building, talking, laughing, training. This had been my home for years now and I loved it, but I loved Angh more. Home was where he was.

"He's mine, Niobe. My mate. I don't care if you approve. I'll still do my job for the I.C., but you can consider this my resignation from the Academy. If you need me, I'll be on The Colony from now on."

"With your mate?"

Duh. "Yes. With Angh."

"I don't think so, Kira. It's too late for that." She turned her back on me and I bit back a snarl of rage that she could be so callous, so calm. So fucking cold. But then I saw where she was headed. A shelf remained intact in the corner. On the top shelf rested an actual glass bottle of vodka from one of the premier distilleries in Russia and three more shot glasses.

When she didn't say anything, I took the mating cuffs I had clipped to my belt and held them up. All four of them.

Shit.

"He went beast, didn't he?" My question was asked softly. It was the voice I used right before I killed my enemies. And right now, the Vice Admiral was dangerously close to making that list. *That* was why her room was destroyed. That was the only reason why he'd have taken off the cuffs. If he'd given up. *Shit.*

"Don't look at me like I've betrayed you, Kira," she countered. "I did not force him to remove the cuffs."

I believed her, but that wasn't the whole story. The destroyed room said a whole lot more. "But you did do something. What did you say to him?"

She gave a slight shrug, took a sip of her drink. "I merely offered him a position, as you well know I had planned to do after speaking with Commander Phan on the last mission. The rest?" She motioned with her drink at the mess that remained in her office. "The rest was his way of refusing the offer."

He wouldn't have destroyed the room just because he didn't want to join the I.C.

"I call bullshit. You can do better than that." Something else had to have happened. There was no way the Atlan warrior I knew would lose his mind like this over a stupid job offer. No. Way.

She slammed back the rest of her vodka and refilled the glass. She held the bottle out to me, offering me a drink. "Vodka? It's from my mother's home country on Earth. There is nothing else like it."

The Vice Admiral was half human? And Russian? She'd be able to drink me under the table...if it still had legs.

"I had plenty of that shit when I was on Earth. I don't want a drink. I want the truth."

She tilted her head toward the door. "Go ask him yourself, Kira. I did nothing. Merely—" She set the vodka back on the shelf and pointed to the cuffs, then to me. "—helped things along."

I stacked the cuffs, heard their clink, felt them warm in my palm as I watched her drink her damn vodka. "If anything happens to him, I'm going to kill you."

Her smile was not friendly. "Are you threatening a superior officer, Captain?"

I shook my head slowly, took the vodka from her hand and slammed back the drink in one motion. The sharp bite of it made me wince and I felt the searing burn work its way down my throat to warm my belly. "No. I'm telling the truth to a woman I thought was my friend."

I held out the glass and she took it, then I turned on my heel and walked away before I did something *really* stupid.

The brig wasn't designed to hold an Atlan in beast mode, and especially not if he was angry.

The best I could hope for was that he wasn't so out of his mind that he wouldn't listen. The worst?

No. I couldn't think about the worst. I just had to hope I got there in time.

Kira, The Brig, Coalition Academy, Zioria

. . .

THE SOUNDS OF THE BEAST'S RAGE REACHED ME BEFORE I was halfway to his cell. It stopped me in my tracks, then spurred me on. He was angry, hurt, upset. Fierce. Whatever the word, the beast was pissed. And I ached for him, and Angh. The energy fields might hold, but the walls and anchors they were built into were not meant to contain a beast.

If Angh was still in there, it was because he wanted to be. And there was only one reason for that, because he saw no reason to escape. To fight. God, it was as if I'd gotten an ion blast to the heart. That hurt almost as much as seeing what they'd done to him.

He was strapped down to a table, the bands around his body so thick they looked like they were preparing to mummify a corpse, not hold down a living being. Somehow, when they'd stunned him and dragged him down here they'd changed him into the light green material of the medical unit. He looked healthy, considering. Thank god. But that meant he was full strength and dangerous.

I'd never seen him like this. Mindless. Roaring. Totally out of control. The sight made my heart break all over again. Last night had been the most painful conversation I'd ever had. To say I wouldn't wear the cuffs or be his had been horrible, but when he'd told me he wouldn't have me, that our love wasn't worth the lives that would be lost... Last night had broken me into a million pieces. We'd both been wrong, for I wasn't the only one to fight. It wasn't up to me to save the world...the universe. I was a mere cog...a good one, but a cog nonetheless. I'd be replaced if I died on a mission. They've have another warrior stepping in to fill my shoes in a matter of hours. But I *could* do my work and be Angh's mate. I wasn't sure why I hadn't seen it sooner, and now, seeing him like this in the brig, was my fault.

The rejection, our agreement, it had broken him, too. And that, too, was my fault. I wasn't the only one who could run the missions and save the world. Save the galaxy.

Hell, I couldn't even save him. My mate. The only man I'd ever loved.

All the things I'd said to him, the reasons I'd thought we couldn't be together were all bullshit. And ego. And me being a fucking coward. I'd done this to him. Not the Vice Admiral. Not the Hive. He'd survived all of them. But he hadn't survived me.

God, I was a bitch.

I might have broken him, brought Angh so low that he lay strapped to a table in the brig, but I could save him. Now. Now that I'd gotten my head out of my ass.

"Open it and get out," I hissed, pointing at the barrier.

"He's lost to the fever, Captain. The Atlans are sending an envoy for him in a matter of hours to decide his fate. From what I've heard, there's a contaminated fighter who came here with him to complete the execution. A human, no less." The Atlan cadet swallowed and there was pain in his eyes, pain for a fallen hero. It seemed he wouldn't become a guard once he was done with the Academy. "I can't let you in there. He's too dangerous."

He stared down at me, way down, shook his head, but there was condemnation in his eyes when he saw the cuffs in my hand. Judgment. He'd grown up with this, of executing those who'd gone into Mating Fever, who couldn't be saved. He knew the drill better than me and yet he was the one who looked upset while I had my inner beast fucking raging.

The four Prillon warriors standing guard with him looked at me like I had lost my mind. Perhaps I had, but it was about damned time. I outranked all of them, plus the young Atlan, and the young Prillon standing at the control panel that would bring down the barrier. I wasn't in the mood for bullshit.

"Open it and get out. That's an order. He's mine. My mate. And I'm not going to ask again."

The Prillons looked to the Atlan for a decision, not because the Atlan outranked them—they were all third-year cadets based on the stripes on their uniforms—but because the Atlan understood what was happening here in a way the others could not.

"He might kill you, Captain," he warned. "He might kill you and not know what he's doing." The Atlan's deep rumbling voice reminded me of Angh's, but it sounded so young and innocent. Naïve. He hadn't seen battle yet. Hadn't survived what my Angh had survived. He was young and fragile. Weak.

Angh was not. He was so strong. Too strong.

"He won't hurt me," I told him. "He's the strongest warrior I've ever known." I took the first small cuff and locked it around my wrist as the guards watched. Their eyes widened at what I was doing. They knew what the cuffs meant, the seriousness of it. Perhaps they'd now take my words just as seriously. "He's mine and I'm here to claim him. Get out of my way."

When the lock on my cuff clicked into place Angh

roared, the sound something I'd never heard before. It was raw and filled with both power and rage. Startled, the Atlan put his hand on my arm to pull me away from the cell. I tried to shrug out of his hold, feeling and savoring the weight and feel of the cuff about my wrist.

I turned to find Angh had turned his head and his beast's eyes were narrowed, focused on the other warrior's huge hand on my arm.

"Get out of here," I commanded. "All of you. He won't hurt me, but he'll kill you without blinking. And get your hand off me. I'm wearing one of his cuffs and you're touching me. Not smart." I stepped forward, closer to the barrier and out of the guard's reach.

The Atlan guard's eyes widened and his hand fell back to his side as if I'd burned him. He just nodded his head to the Prillon at the controls when the first strap holding Angh down snapped. The sound was loud, like the sudden breaking of a large tree limb, and I realized the bindings truly weren't going to contain him. Not now that he'd seen me, seen another male touch me. I had hoped to get up there and put his cuffs back on his wrists, give him a few minutes to calm down, to soothe his beast, and then let him get up slowly.

Unfortunately, it looked like that wasn't going to be an option. I would be dealing with Angh in full beast mode. I just had to hope he was still in there somewhere. The beast knew me...hopefully.

I waved at all of the guards behind my back, unwilling to turn away or break eye contact with the beast who was determined to come for me. Slowly, deliberately, I lifted the second small cuff to my wrist and snapped it in place as Angh watched. There. Done. I was his. I knew the cuffs could come off, but I wouldn't remove mine. Ever. I'd made my decision. They were staying on.

He snarled and broke three more straps. *Ping. Ping. Ping.* He'd be free in seconds and the walls wouldn't hold him. "Lower the barrier and get out of here. Now."

Finally, the guards listened. The buzzing, electrical force field energy that had been in place disappeared and there was nothing but empty air and a few short steps separating me from my mate. But I waited, stood in place until the clomping of the guards' boots was gone and I knew we were alone.

I knew this place was monitored on vid feeds, but I didn't care at the moment. Angh needed me and it didn't matter who watched as long as they were somewhere else, somewhere a raging beast couldn't literally tear them in half.

"Angh. I'm so sorry." My voice was gentle, but loud, hopefully both beast and Atlan could hear me. He was in full beast mode. Huge. While he wasn't standing, I knew him to be eight feet tall. Muscles on top of muscles. Clenched fists. Ragged breathing. Intense gaze.

"Mine."

The beast uttered one word, his eyes focused on me like lasers, and I knew the question of whether or not he still wanted me had been answered. But how far gone was he? Was he going to hurt me? I'd acted bravely, assured the guards that he would never do so. And I had to believe that. I had to, or this wasn't going to work.

"You're mine, Angh," I told him, lifting my arms up in front of me like Wonder Woman and her bulletproof bracelets. "Do you see these cuffs on my wrists? I claim you, Warlord Anghar of Atlan. You better get yourself under control, Warlord, because you've got a mate who needs you."

"Mine."

The remaining straps broke over his chest and he sat, ripping the rest to shreds in a matter of seconds. Then he was up, stalking toward me like a conqueror, his bare chest magnificent. The green medical pants were soft and did absolutely nothing to hide the huge cock already straining to reach me. Thick and long, I knew what it felt like inside me. Filling me, stretching me. But that had been just sex. I hadn't had on the cuffs. Now, I had the obvious proof that I wanted him. That while he kept saying I was his, he was also mine

I knew what this beast wanted. And my entire body responded, my pussy flooding with wet welcome and my blood heating with anticipation. Yes, I wanted it, too. God, I needed it. To know he was right there with me in this. That we were both wild, frantic and desperate to mate. To claim. I wanted his mark, to belong to him and no one else.

This was a beast coming to claim me, not a male. He was huge, nothing remotely civilized in his eyes or his stance. There would be no gentle wooing or soft words like the night before. He was raw. Untamed. Completely wild. This was different. I'd pushed him to the brink, and I would take what he needed for me to be claimed.

And I was so damn hot for him my knees almost buckled on the spot. I wanted him to lift me up against the wall and bury himself balls deep. I wanted him pumping into me like a madman, savage and so hot he burned us both. To groan and grunt, to be fucked by his inner beast until I forgot any male's name but his. To *feel* the claim in my pussy for days. Forever.

I took a deep breath and held out my hand to stop him when he was just two steps away.

Thank God he stopped, his chest heaving, but I knew then that he was still in there. My Angh. He wasn't a mindless beast. Wild, yes, but he was still mine.

"You're not touching me again until you're mine, Angh. Until these cuffs are back where they belong." I dangled them between us, the ones he'd shed to set me free. But neither of us would be free until he out them back on.

Instead of taking them from me, as I expected, he simply held out both arms and waited for me to place them on his wrists. I hadn't thought about it too much when I locked the smaller cuffs around my own wrists, but now I realized the weight of the moment. This was more than a wedding ring. More than a simple marriage would have been back on Earth. This was truly forever. Live together. Fight together. Die together. These cuffs were never coming off my wrists. I didn't care if we couldn't be more than fifty feet apart or we'd be zapped with pain. I had seen what would happen to him now, the risk he took, and I was never going to risk him like that again.

He was giving himself to me, just as he'd had that first night we'd met. I hadn't understood then, but I did now. If I died first, he'd follow me, his beast unable to survive without a mate to soothe him. Where I went, he would follow. He would fight for me, kill for me, die for me.

I realized, as I locked the first cuff around his wrist, that I was more than willing to do the same for him.

"I love you, Angh." I reached for the second wrist, the cuff the final step in claiming this magnificent male for myself. I didn't care about consequences. Not anymore. I only cared about him. "I should have told you before. I should have put your cuffs on last night. I'm so sorry."

I snapped the final cuff in place and still Angh didn't move, it was like he was a stone wall, that if he moved a single inch, he would crumble.

I held my breath.

This was so not going like I thought it would. He was supposed to be kissing me now. Passionate and wild and totally out of control, not staring me down like I'd just killed his favorite puppy.

He was strong, disciplined, at least enough to hold himself back, and he was hurt. Hurting. I'd broken his heart and I hated myself for it. He'd been prepared to *die* because of me.

And so I would continue to lead this, to lead us to through the claiming. The cuffs were on, but there was still more to go. Reaching for the edge of my armored shirt, I lifted it over my head and dropped it to the ground. The undershirt followed, and the unusual sports bra I wore beneath that.

Angh's breathing increased in speed, but his gaze still didn't leave mine as I finished undressing, kicking off my boots and stepping out of my pants until I stood naked before him, wearing nothing but the cuffs. His cuffs. Without them, I could be fully clothed and yet I would be bare. They were all I needed now.

When he still just stared, I walked toward him and wrapped my arms around him. Chest to chest. His flimsy hospital pants the only thing separating us. I felt every hard inch of him, the thickness of his cock, the heat from his skin, the beast's bulging muscles. I didn't know what else to say. What else to do.

"Please. Please forgive me for being so damn stupid."

With a growl, he spun me around, my back pressed to his chest, and carried me to the wall where a large metal bracket I hadn't noticed before was imbedded. I gasped at the speed with which he moved, but didn't fight him. He lifted my wrists and placed them over the metal, somehow activating them so I was stuck, on my tip-toes, arms over my head. Strung up and totally at his mercy.

"Mine." The beast growled in my ear and I turned my head to watch as he ripped the flimsy hospital pants off his body and dropped them to the floor. He was naked, his cock huge and hard and dripping with pre-cum. My pussy flooded with heat, the wetness coating my thighs. I wanted him. Hard and hot and up against the wall. Right now.

"Yes," I breathed. "You're mine, Angh. My mate. Fuck me. Do it. I need you. Claim me." I twisted and turned, trying to free my hands so I could turn around and touch him. Kiss him.

But he was in control now, and he had no intention of letting me have my way. This was how it was supposed to happen. Perhaps not in a brig, but rough and wild, the female at the male's mercy. The beast's mercy. This was the one time the beast was allowed to take complete control over the man, claiming me so that it could be soothed, so the Mating Fever could be gone.

"Ready?" The beast stepped behind me, his cock pressed to the small of my back, his huge hands cupping my breasts, not with tenderness, but massaging them like he wanted to devour me. All of me.

Seconds later, one hand dropped to my clit, slid past it and slipped deep, testing my wetness, my readiness for him.

"Angh!" My head fell back, onto his chest, and I squirmed, tried to press my clit against his rough palm, tried to fuck his finger. But I had no leverage, no way to move, no way to do anything but take what he gave me. It felt so good, a searing heat so powerful I would come if he just touched me...more.

When he lifted my hips and filled me from behind in one strong thrust, I nearly came. So big. So thick. I rippled and clenched around him trying to adjust. He was *almost* too much, but I would take him. All of him. Every hard, thick inch. I wanted him so much, so damn much. This was the first time we were really together, as mates. This was everything that had been missing before and I realized I had always been holding back, just a little. Just enough. I needed it wild. I needed it rough. I needed it out of my control.

"Mine." His growl made my pussy clamp down on him like a fist and his beast groaned the exact moment I did.

He used his hands to reach around to the front of my thighs and spread me open, my wetness there catching on his palms, coating them. I slipped down a bit farther, took more of him, the thick head of his cock bumping the top of my pussy with a relentless, teasing pressure that built and built inside me until I thought I would explode if he didn't move. This was it. My everything. He was in me, claiming me. I was his and he would never let me forget it.

Angh

I CAME TO MYSELF SLOWLY, THE BEAST NONE TOO WILLING to share control when we were exactly where we wanted to be, balls deep in our mate, the mating cuffs on her wrists, her hot, wet core wrapped around us like a fist. Clenching, squeezing, milking the seed from my balls.

I'd heard every word she said, the beast all too eager to ignore the threat the Vice Admiral had made and just take what it wanted. Kira.

With a supreme effort, I'd held him back. I knew taking her would be wrong. Bad. But the beast wouldn't listen. I prevented him from ruling us both until she'd taken off her clothes and the smell of her wet heat filled my head with a lust so powerful there was no stopping the Mating Fever, or my beast, from taking what was his. Ours.

Her. Our mate.

Appeased, the beast finally allowed me to share some space in our head. Now, we teased her. Pumped in and out of her body slowly. She was helpless, submissive, trusting me and the beast not to hurt her.

The feeling was powerful, heady, and I knew Kira was everything to me. Everything.

I would fuck her. Fill her with my seed. Claim her.

And I'd do what I had to do to keep her safe. If that meant eliminating the Vice Admiral, so be it. No one was going to use us against one another. No one. And with the cuffs about our wrists, no one would doubt.

I'd kill the fucking king on Prillon Prime or the leader of my home world, if I had to.

I wanted this to last forever, our connection, the sweet, blissful feel of being deep inside her, but the smell of her skin, the softness of her pressing against my chest, the softness of her ass as it bounced against my hips was too much. Her wet core pulsing. Coaxing. The orgasm built, drawing up into my balls in a blissfully painful twist, and I knew I wouldn't last, needed to take her with me.

I dropped one hand to her clit, found her swollen and slick and stroked her, increasing my speed, pumping into her like the primitive animal she turned me into.

Her scream was my cue to let go, and her pussy milked me as my roar filled the entire lower level of the Academy building where they'd held me.

I coated her pussy with my seed until it overflowed, slipping down her thighs, over my balls. I'd marked her. There was no going back. The claiming was complete.

The Mating Fever was instantly gone. My beast was soothed.

Hot, sweaty, barely breathing, I held her there, pressed to the wall as my beast settled, completely content for the first time in years. Hell, I never recalled being this sated, this much at peace.

Lowering my head to her shoulder, I kissed her there, gently. Finally, *gently.* I knew my voice would be hoarse, but I had to say it. "I love you, Kira. You're mine."

I saw her smile as I brushed her damp hair back from her face. "I love you, too. You're my beast now, Angh. No more of this dying bullshit, okay? You scared the hell out of me."

The bliss I'd felt dimmed. She'd only come here

because she thought I was going to die. She hadn't chosen me, she'd chosen not to let me die.

Before I could process that, someone cleared their throat.

Instantly, I moved my body to block the other's view. But that was all I could do. The cuffs were still activated, holding her wrists locked to the wall above her head. And my cock was still buried deep. I didn't want to pull out. Not yet.

If I was honest, I wanted to stay there forever.

With Kira sheltered from the stranger's eyes, I turned my head to find the Vice Admiral standing with her arms crossed over her chest and a victorious grin on her face.

"Now that you've got that sorted out, finish up and be in Transport 2 in an hour."

I growled, the beast coming from deep within me, taking control. It was no longer raging out of control, but fierce and focused.

"Kill you."

This was the person who had threatened our mate and the beast was angry.

The Vice Admiral didn't bat an eye at the threat. "Yes, well, can you do it after you get back from Sector 54? You're mated now. You will go together. Fight together. I'm counting on the two of you to be my strongest team and we've got an I.C. asset that needs immediate extraction. So, one hour."

With that, she turned on her heel and took three steps. Stopped. Faced me again. "Oh, and in case you were wondering, I relieved the guards monitoring the prison cell vid feeds, and a certain period of time will be mysteriously missing from Academy data." With that, she left me alone with my mate. Both beast and man at a complete and total loss for words.

Was that the same woman who'd had me sent to the brig, strapped to the table and being readied for execution? Had this been her master plan all along? Was Kira here because she truly loved me, or because this manipulative female had forced Kira's hand?

I couldn't think on it now, for my cock was still hard, the vids were down and we were still alone. We might have to head to Sector 54, but I'd fuck my mate once more before we did so. This time, I would be in control, not my beast. But Kira would come again. Her pussy would pulse and spasm as I watched. I wanted to see her face this time. She was mine to pleasure. Mine to tame. And even if she had only come here to save my life, the beast didn't care about the rules. He didn't care about the Vice Admiral's schemes. He'd taken what was offered and it was too late to change anything.

Kira was mine now, whether she truly wanted to be or not.

And I wasn't strong enough to let her go.

13

*A*ngh, *Sector 54, Hive Integration Unit Outpost, Prisoner Cell Block*

I HEARD THE HIVE DRONES. THEY WERE EVERYWHERE. What was normally a random buzzing sound in the back of my mind was now full-blown conversations between Hive trios moving around the base.

I understood everything. Every. Word.

"Do you hear that?" Crouched next to me in the side corridor was my beautiful, courageous mate in full battle gear, ion rifle out and ready. She looked fierce, professional, and so fucking sexy I had a hard time keeping my eyes off her. I'd never thought of anyone as being *sexy* while behind enemy lines, but there was a first for everything.

Behind us, a small strike force of human, Everian and Viken fighters waited for orders from their leader. Kira. Not me. ReCon teams were normally made up of warriors from the smaller races. They could get in, get out, and move quickly in tight spaces. I was a novelty here, and they looked at me like I was a clumsy giant, despite the fact that I could kill them with one strike of my bare fists. So I ignored them.

Kira was here. I went where she did. End of discussion.

Our target to extract, a Rogue 5 weapons specialist and secret I.C. operative from the Styx legion, was supposed to be located on the second level, on the far end of the cell block. How the Vice Admiral had come by her information, I had no idea and I knew she wouldn't tell us if I asked.

There was only one way in and one way out of that corridor. The back of the prison section was made up of stone several hundred feet thick. We had transport beacons, but had no idea if they would work this deep underground. The beacons had been tested in tunnels on other worlds, but never this far beneath the surface.

This meant we had to break him out and get him to the surface. Alive or dead. Those were our orders. We couldn't allow the Hive to break into his mind.

I cursed under my breath and shook my head to clear it of the racket the Hive drones were making. There were nine Hive on this outpost. Three trios. And I could hear every single one of them like they were standing next to me.

The Hive did love their dark, desolate caves.

"Warlord?" Kira's whisper made me lean down to hear her, but I didn't take my eyes off the corridor before us, or lower my weapon. There were seven of us, but if the Hive discovered our presence, they'd swarm our position, lock down the exits and transport drones in by the dozens until we were trapped.

That was not happening. I'd die before I allowed them to capture me again. Or Kira. No fucking way would they get her.

"Yes, Captain?" I addressed her with respect, because I expected the other warriors with us to do the same.

"Do you hear that?" She pivoted in her crouched position to address the others. "Do any of you hear that?"

"Hear what?" The Viken warrior closest to her shrugged. "I don't hear anything."

"That buzzing." She knocked on her helmet, just over the ear, where the comm link would be. "I think my comm is going out."

I returned my full attention to the seemingly deserted corridors ahead of us. The Hive were moving, a trio heading in our direction, coming for the prisoner we were here to recover. How I knew that, *why* I knew that, I refused to think about.

I clenched my fists as the beast raged, the cuffs the only thing holding him in check. We were with our mate. We had to protect her. Nothing else, not even the rage and pain of torture creatures like these had inflicted on me, mattered now.

Kira mattered. And the mission mattered to her. That was all. My only reason for existence. The Vice Admiral was smart, her strategy worthy of the best in the galaxy. She had gotten what she wanted. I had what I wanted. But Kira? I just didn't know.

Had she really chosen me? Or had the Vice Admiral forced her hand? Or—

The beast howled at me to shut the fuck up and go rip

up the Hive Soldiers coming down the hall. For once, I agreed with him. Anything to rid my mind of the thoughts circling like hungry carrion.

"Three Hive approaching, left corridor."

Kira whipped back around and raised her rifle. "How long?"

"Now."

The Hive Soldier who rounded the corner first was once a Prillon, big and mean, his entire face was silver. His eyes solid metal, like Denzel's. There was nothing left of the warrior he'd once been and when he spoke, his voice was monotone. Mechanical and empty. "Intruders. Level—"

His head was bloody pulp in my hand where I'd smashed it into the wall. But the other two took up the call before I could finish the job.

"Level Two. Intruders on Level Two."

Ion rifle fire came around me from behind and took down the remaining Soldiers, Kira's cursing flying from her lips almost too quickly for my NPU to keep up.

"What the fuck, Angh? We wait for them to pass, strike from behind. Get in. Get out. Don't get caught. Got it?"

The Viken behind her was laughing when I turned around, the Prillon's lifeless body still dangling from my hand, forgotten. "That is not how Atlan's normally approach battle."

She sighed. "This isn't battle, this is ReCon."

"Then I will study ReCon strategies when we return."

"*This* is why Atlans aren't on ReCon teams." Grinning at me now, I knew all was forgiven and her gaze dropped to the Hive hanging from my grip. "You done killing that one? I'd like to get our target and get out of here."

I dropped the Hive like a stone at my feet and moved in the direction she indicated, down the corridor leading to the prisoner from Rogue 5, the man with information in his head so valuable to the I.C. they were willing to sacrifice all of our lives to keep it out of Hive hands.

Finding his cell was easy. The locked door was hinged metal with bolts imbedded in the cave's rock walls. Pathetic.

I tore it off its hinges just as easily as I'd done to Kira's classroom door and stepped aside so someone from the team could go in. I was half beast, as he'd refused to remain dormant when there was so much fun to be had, and I knew if I walked into that prison cell, the poor male would likely have a heart attack.

I held the door to the side as Kira and the Viken walked by me. He grinned. "And *that* is why Atlans should be on every mission."

"Shut up, Farren," Kira snapped at him, tapping the side of her helmet again, but her words only made the other members of the team laugh.

"Rokk? I'm with ReCon. We're getting you out of here."

Moments later, the large warrior stumbled into the hallway leaning heavily on Kira and the Viken, his arms wrapped around their shoulders. Rokk was weak and battered. Nearly naked, the remnants of torn pants barely covered him. His skin was coated in dried blood. But I knew the Hive hadn't started the true torture yet, as I saw no Hive implants on his body, no silver pieces burrowing into his flesh like living parasites.

The beast wanted to howl at the memories and I held him back by force of will. It should have been easy to control him, now that I had a mate. But he was like me, frustrated and unsure.

Did our mate truly want us? Did it matter?

Fuck yes. It did. And until we knew for sure, the beast wouldn't calm completely, and neither would I.

I watched them stumble for a few steps under his heavy weight as the bastard looked to be part Atlan and part Hyperion, the strange fangs in his mouth all the evidence I needed that he belonged to that primitive species. His body was covered with a significant number of tattoos, each one of them in a language I didn't recognize.

Kira saw my interest. "They're names, Angh. Names of the people he is sworn to protect. The names of his people. The higher their rank in Styx legion, the more names they have inked into their flesh."

My respect for the alien warrior grew as I noticed hundreds of names swirling down his torso, covering a large portion of his back and chest. He caught me looking as well, so I asked. "How many?"

"Two hundred and thirty-four. I'm only a lieutenant."

I grunted at that. "Leave him to me."

With a shrug, the Viken stepped aside and I took his place. When I had him, I nodded at Kira and she, too stepped aside. Rokk was big, but no larger than an average Prillon. If he were Atlan, it was only half, and I'd carried many brothers off the battlefield without assistance. "Go. I will do this."

With one last glance, Kira nodded, trusting me, and took off back down the way we came. Farren, the Viken who seemed to be her closest ally, was with her, running formation. Checking corners. There was no need. I could hear them. All of them. That didn't keep me from panicking having her farther than arm's reach. She couldn't go far from me, thank fuck, because of the cuffs and that soothed my beast.

"There are three Soldiers and three Scouts coming. Half on the left and other half blocking our exit."

"Fuck. How do you know that?" The two ReCon members behind me cursed but didn't argue, moving ahead with their weapons. But I stopped them.

"No. Take him. I will deal with the Hive."

"Yes, sir." They weren't new recruits, and they weren't stupid. They had seen what an Atlan in beast mode could do in battle. And since this was no longer a stealth op, thanks to me, I would clean up the mess.

I handed the prisoner off to them and ran forward, a bellow of challenge ringing ahead of me in the halls. I would draw them to me and allow the rest of the team to pick them off with ion rifles, one by one.

"Damn it, Angh!" Kira yelled, but I had been in more battles than she would ever know. I knew the Hive well, how they worked. How they thought. I'd been one of them and the rage I felt toward their kind still simmered.

They waited in the branching corridors where we'd been a few short minutes ago. Ion fire blasted into me, behind me. I was surrounded, but I charged through all of it toward the first group, ripping them to pieces with my bare hands and not worrying where the others were. I'd finish these three, and move to the next. And the next.

My beast was howling with fury, the killing frenzy, the need to ensure our mate was protected making him especially vicious.

The first three were dead, the fury of battle gone, and my beast turned to look for our next opponent.

"Angh! Grenade!" Kira's warning rang through the space as a small, metallic device landed in the center of the room.

Kira was running. She dove, throwing her body over the grenade as the rest of her team dove for cover. She actually curled her body around it, twisted to place her back between me and the explosive.

Holy fucking— Protecting me. Saving *me.*

"No!" The beast roared. I roared. I panicked. I had seen this weapon before, hundreds of times. I knew exactly what it was and what it would do to my mate, how it would tear her body into pieces.

The Hive were gone, retreating far enough to escape the blast.

Silence.

Kira was on the ground, panting. Curled around the grenade.

Nothing.

"What the fuck?" Farren cautiously slid forward on hands and knees, closer to Kira, but I was there first, reaching for her.

"No! Don't touch her!" The Hyperion's voice was crisp, a clear command. "Don't disrupt the frequency or it'll explode."

I turned to him, frustrated at how difficult it was to speak. She was curled around a fucking grenade. "Why?"

Kira rolled slowly, the armed grenade flashing with a strange blue light as she held it up, close to her head. "I can hear them."

I froze in place and forced myself to calm, to *listen.*

She was right. I could hear them, too. And I could hear *it*, the weapon, the explosive. Rokk explained as she looked up at him. "They're new Hive tech, designed to recognize one of their own. They were losing a lot of Soldiers in battle, so they've made advanced modifications to their weaponry."

"Their bombs know if the target is Hive or not?" Farren asked, eyes wide with surprise.

"Yes." Rokk looked at Kira. "And for some reason, it thinks you're one of them."

She looked up at me and our gazes locked. We knew; we both knew exactly why it wasn't going off. Somehow, the added connection had linked our minds, the communication even clearer than what I'd experienced with Chloe and the mine field around Battleship Karter. And that connection was protecting us.

Holy fuck. We'd had a connection, my mate and I, but that was on a personal level. Now, together, we were connected to hear the Hive as well.

If we could use this knowledge on the battlefield, broadcast Hive signal and destabilize their weapons, it would be a huge advantage in the war.

Kira held out her hand to me and I pulled her up slowly so she didn't jostle the grenade. "They don't know what to do. Let's get out of here now, before they figure something out."

I looked at Rokk. "Apologies, but I don't have time to argue with you." With that, I lifted the heavy male over my shoulder and started running, the rest of the team falling in step.

The Scouts who blocked the entrance were easy targets, not as large or fast as the Soldiers down below in the caves, and I grunted in approval as Farren and the others made quick work of them.

We ran, the Hyperion grunting each time his gut landed on my shoulder, but I couldn't afford to be gentle. He'd survived the Hive, he'd just have to suffer the journey back to our transport location.

Kira spotted a smaller cave entrance, one positioned to block the main force of the blast, and she threw the grenade as she sprinted. Tossed and ran. Shit. A second later, the explosion rocked the ground, but we kept moving.

Get in. Get out. Don't get caught.

Her words rang in my ears until we reached the extraction point and I dropped the Hyperion on the ground in a heap.

I was reaching for her when the transport energy surrounded us, tore us into pieces and put us back together on the other side.

A medical team swarmed the transport pad back on Zioria and I recognized Transport 2 at the Academy. Elsewhere on the grounds, business went on as usual, as if the Hive battle had never happened. Classes. Training. And all the while, the most important missions in the war were being completed right under the cadets' noses.

Vice Admiral Niobe was waiting for us as well, her smile genuine when she saw Rokk. "Lieutenant. I'm glad to see you made it."

His only response was a grunt of pain as the medics lifted him onto a medical stretcher to take him for whatever healing he needed in a ReGen pod.

I ignored all of them, my eyes only on my mate. "Kira."

She turned from greeting the Vice Admiral and

congratulating her team on a job well done. She did all the things she was supposed to do, the things a leader would do.

But she hadn't thrown herself on that grenade for her team. She hadn't positioned her body to shield them from the blast. She'd done that for me. And she was going to get a fucking spanking for that.

"Kira." The beast spoke now, unhappy with the wait. We were furious with her for risking her life that way. And humbled. Her love wasn't fabricated or manipulated. It was real. So fucking real she'd thrown herself on a grenade to save me.

She must have heard the tone of my voice, for she walked to me but didn't say a word, just wrapped her arms around my waist and snuggled into my chest. Our weapons bumped and our armor was in the way, but she was warm and alive and in my arms. It calmed my beast as nothing else could as I digested the truth.

She loved me. Would kill for me. Fight beside me.

Die for me. This part didn't sit well with either me or my beast, but I would talk with her about it later. She might fight beside me, but that didn't mean she took ridiculous risks, like falling on a fucking grenade. Yes, a spanking would definitely be in order.

I would have held her for hours, content just to hold her, but the Vice Admiral walked to stand beside us.

"Still want to kill me, Warlord?"

I grunted, but the woman had earned my respect. "Not at the moment."

"Good, because you'll not be staying."

"What?" Kira lifted her head and I placed my hands on her shoulders to hold her back. Seemed I wasn't the only one still a bit angry with the Vice Admiral and her meddling.

"We need you on one of the Karter's outer ships in Sector 216 as soon as possible."

Kira's shoulders slumped and I knew I was not going to get a chance to rest. And spank her ass. And fuck. And sleep. And feast on my mate's pussy. Fill her with my cock. Sleep. Eat. Massage every inch of her in warm bath oils. Plans. I had plans and the Vice Admiral was getting in the way of every one of them.

"When do we leave?" I asked, my teeth gritting together.

The Vice Admiral checked her wrist comm. "You have an hour."

"Great," Kira mumbled, but she was speaking to an empty room. The Vice Admiral was already gone.

ngh, Planet Vesper, Helios Retreat

"This is not the flank ship in Sector 216," I commented, turning in a slow circle, taking in our surroundings. This was *not* a transport room.

Kira was beside me, which meant I wasn't losing my mind. She began to laugh and I had to question whether she'd lost hers.

"Toto, we're not in Kansas anymore," she replied, although I had no idea what the hell she was talking about.

I gripped her arm, suddenly panicked, then tugged her behind me. She stumbled, but I held on as I wrapped my arm about her, holding her against my back. My beast came to the front and I felt it taking over. It wasn't the fever, but beast mode. "Was our transport intercepted? We have no weapons." My beast was the only weapon I had.

"Angh, calm down. Tell your beast to chill the fuck out." I felt her hand as she patted my back.

"Calm down? What does getting cold have to do with anything? Where the *fuck* are we? How did we get here? The flank ship should have the blackness of space out of the portals, not land. Sand. A green sky." I walked closer to the large doorway, which was open to the warm air, pulling Kira along with me. "And two suns. In order for us to see two suns, then we have to be about...three light years from Sector 216."

"All I can see is the back of your shirt," she grumbled. Kira pushed out of my hold, but only because I let her, but I didn't let her go far. "It's beautiful here. I've never seen two suns before."

I looked down at her, frowning. "Out of everything I just said, you're focused on the number of suns?"

She smiled. "Yes." Turning, she took a step out of the doorway, but I grabbed her about the waist. "Angh, we're at some kind of resort or hotel, not in Hive territory. We're definitely not on a battleship. Look, there's a pool."

I followed the direction of her hand as she pointed. There was a pool, the colored tiles making the water look deep blue.

Kira spun about. "We're in a bedroom, not a prison, not a transport room. The bed is built for an Atlan. See?" She pointed again.

"Warlord Anghar, Captain Dahl, greetings."

I spun about at the words that came from behind us. I had the male in a grip about his neck and had him lifted two feet off the ground, his body pressed against the doorframe before Kira even gasped in surprise.

"Who the fuck are you?" I asked, my voice booming.

Kira came over, tugged on my elbow as the male's eyeballs began to bulge, his pale face turning purple. His hands gripped and tugged at my forearm, but was absolutely no match for my beast.

"Let him down!" Kira shouted.

"He is a threat."

The man dropped one hand and slapped it against the wall until the room's comms unit came to life.

"Surprise!" Cadet Melody's perky voice had me turning my head, loosening my hold on the male.

"Angh, put the poor man down. He works here."

"Here? Like I said, where the fuck is here?" I narrowed my gaze at him as he put a hand to his neck and coughed. His normal coloring was returning. He wasn't Atlan, didn't have the darker skin tone of a Prillon. I had no idea what his home planet was.

"Will you stop saying fuck?" Kira asked.

"Hi, Kira and Angh!" Melody's face took up most of the comm display. Denzel was behind her, arms crossed in his familiar stance, although he was smiling. *Smiling.*

"I know you're probably freaking out. Don't panic. Really. I heard about your mating in the brig—not very romantic—and talked with Vice Admiral Niobe and told her she wasn't a very good matchmaker. Newly-mated couples need candles, wine, romance, not prison walls and conjugal sex for their claiming. Sheesh." Melody rolled her eyes, clearly disappointed in the Vice Admiral. "Anyway, she cleared it with Governor Rone on The Colony and we rerouted your transport. You're at the Helios Retreat for your honeymoon!"

She was excited. Too excited for another couple's leave for a *honeymoon*. I wasn't familiar with Earth's suns and moons and so I had no idea why it was called honey. I gave up trying to understand all the Earth slang after spending so much time with Denzel. As for her exuberance, I didn't understand that either, but the surprised and pleased look on Kira's face told me she did.

I eyed the male before me who'd surprised us, who clearly was an employee of the retreat. It was obvious now with his black pants and green shirt that had an unusual graphic on the chest with the word Helios below. He eyed me with fear, but hadn't moved or fled, and I was impressed with their level of service. I angled my head out the door and he bolted.

I took a deep breath, then another. I took in my surroundings with a calmer demeanor. *Helios Retreat.* I'd never heard of it, nor Vesper. But, I knew of retreats around the galaxy that many used for vacation. I hadn't been on a vacation in years, not since before I became a Warlord. Before battle. Before the Hive. The idea of being someplace where there was no war, no danger, most likely not even talk of the Hive, was strange.

Crossing my arms over my chest, I turned my attention back to the screen.

Denzel put his hand on Melody's shoulder and she calmed down a bit. "You're on Planet Vesper, nowhere near the battlefront," he said, then kissed her temple, clearly the sign to let her continue.

"Yeah, you're not anywhere near the Hive and the flank battleship thing was all a lie. Don't panic."

"I'm sure it's too late, love," Denzel said. "Knowing Angh, he went all beast mode."

Kira looked up at me. She had her lips rolled between her teeth as if she was trying not to smile.

"Sorry if we made you panic," Melody said with impressive seriousness, just before she clapped her hands together. "We fooled you both. Ha! I guess it helped to have the Vice Admiral involved. I swear, for a half-human, she's no fun. As for you two, you've earned some fun. Three days of suns, sand and sex."

Being sent here was a… present? A gift from Melody and the Governor? And they'd gotten approval from Commander Karter *and* the Vice Admiral? They'd all been in on it? Suns, sand and sex?

I didn't give a shit about the first two, but sex? For three days? My beast circled, then laid down. Content. My cock, however, rose to attention. It was all for three days of being buried deep inside Kira.

"Your return transport is in three days at zero eight hundred. Be ready."

Denzel leaned in again. "Be dressed because your coordinates are pre-loaded and wherever the fuck you are, whatever the fuck you're doing, including fucking…is how you'll transport back. Fair warning. While Kira sure is fine, I have no interest in seeing a pale Atlan ass."

Denzel winked one silver eye.

"Speaking of fucking…" he tugged Melody away from the comms screen and all we could see was a generic officer's quarters. But Melody's giggling could be heard along with, "Show me that big cock," before the comm ended.

I stared down at Kira. Kira stared up at me. "I didn't need to hear the last," she said, then burst out laughing. "Three days," she said, tapping her finger to her lip. I couldn't miss the way her cuff picked up the brightness from the suns. "Whatever shall we do?"

I reached out, stroked her hair, then let it slide down to her shoulder and lower still over the curve of her breast. "I vote for sex," I said.

She laughed. I loved that sound, so open, so...happy. And the look on her face was something I always longed for. None of the tension or worry of her job. No students to lead, no battles to fight. No cares. No worries.

I didn't need a retreat to enjoy my mate; I just needed privacy. A bed wasn't even required. But seeing Kira relaxed and carefree was a side benefit. Perhaps we did need this time away, this time alone where we could be reminded life wasn't all about fighting the Hive. There was peace out there, proof positive that our work was doing good, keeping places like Vesper an escape.

Thanks were in order for those involved in arranging this. Kira was smiling because of it, but it was my job now to keep her that way.

Her pupils dilated; her breathing picked up. "I vote for sex, too."

My beast perked right up and was telling me *Yes. I vote for sex, too. Lots of it.*

Kira stepped closer, put her hand on my chest and pushed. I stepped back and she pushed again until she was walking me backward. She was smiling, so I kept on going. I felt the bed against the back of my calves and with one final push, I dropped to sit on the edge. The mattress was soft. Plush.

Her smile was all for me now. But I wanted her to wear that and nothing else.

My hands went to the bottom of her uniform shirt, curled into the hem.

She stepped back, but her smile didn't slip. "It's my turn to be in charge."

Her voice was soft, yet husky. The blood that was left in my brain traveled to my cock. *Fuck, I loved my mate.*

Her cheeks turned a pretty shade of pink and her eyes flared with heat. "And since I'm a teacher, we're going to start with a very special lesson. Take off your shirt, Warlord."

"Yes, ma'am," I replied, only too willing to follow any order that ended up with fewer clothes on. Once it was on the floor, I waited for her next command, although it needed to happen fast or the beast was going to lose interest in this game and do what he did – fuck her until she screamed my name.

"If I'm going to teach you a lesson, then I need to know you've come prepared." She lifted her shirt up and over her head, letting it fall to the floor. "Have you?"

Her pale hair swung along her back, but I paid it barely any attention. Her breasts, while covered in a simple white bra, were right in front of my face.

"Warlord," she reminded.

I forgot the question. "Ma'am?"

"Have you come prepared?" She tapped her booted foot on the tile floor as if she were irritated by having to repeat herself. I bit the inside of my cheek to keep from smiling. While it had made me hot watching her in action on the practice field at the Academy, and beside her as we fought the Hive, the balance of power was skewed now. This play made my balls ache. This *was* play. I could have her beneath me, cock cramming her full in seconds. But no. I wanted her to have this power over me. I gave it to her, a gift I knew she enjoyed. She owned me, all of me.

And that was a power I had never given another, not my commanders on the battlefield or the people on my home world. Only her.

I was eager—no, desperate—to see where this would go. I knew the end would be what we both wanted. What we needed. It wasn't the destination now. It was all about the journey. And as long as I took it with Kira, I would be one happy Atlan.

Finally.

———

Kira

I'D THINK ABOUT WHAT MELODY AND CHLOE HAD DONE later. I'd check out the pool and the desert and the suns. Later. The only thing I was going to check out now was Angh's cock as he opened up his pants and pulled it out.

I licked my lips. Oh yeah. That was the cock I wanted. Needed. Ached for. I was wet and Angh would find out soon enough. Not yet, though. I had a feeling as soon as he got his hands—literally—on my pussy, our game would be over. And I wanted to play with both man and beast. I saw the primitive lust inside him, the beast watching me with hooded eyes, waiting to pounce. To conquer. To claim.

He could snap at any moment and the thought thrilled me until my pussy was soaking through my clothing. It was like trying to tame a lion. A total rush. A rush I knew would end with orgasm after orgasm until I was so wrung out I literally couldn't move.

Last time I'd been in that condition, Angh had put his mouth on me and made me come again anyway with that skilled tongue.

I whimpered, then stifled it by crossing my arms over my chest—which didn't make me look too superior since I was in just my bra—and said, "Yes, you have come *very well* prepared."

His cock was huge. Atlans were big everywhere. My inner walls clenched, remembering how it felt to be opened up by it, to have that big crown slide over every nerve ending. I'd never been one to come from just penetration alone, but Angh got me there. Sure, my clit was still my magic button, but it seemed my g-spot, which had been hiding my whole life, decided to come join the party with Angh and…holy hell. Coming from the way he pressed and rubbed, slid and stroked over my g-spot was enough to have me speaking in tongues. And I had an NPU that translated it all.

A bead of pre-cum appeared at the tip and Angh's thumb slid over it, captured it. I crooked my finger and he lifted his hand, held the glistening tip up. Leaning forward, I licked it off, the salty tang of it bursting on my tongue, sucking the tip into my mouth. My mouth watered, remembering the feel of his cock there instead, thick and hard as it went deep, opening my throat.

I took his wrist, held him by the mating cuff and pulled his thumb free. I stepped close. "Undress me."

This command he didn't have to be told twice. I was naked and directly before him in seconds. While the air wasn't cold—in fact, it was warm and dry, reminding me of Arizona or spring in Las Vegas—my nipples hardened.

I'd waited long enough. While Angh had taken me

against the wall in the brig on Zioria, it had been quick, hard and wild. His beast had been as much in control as Angh had. I'd loved it. Every hot second of it. That had been elemental and almost desperate. His beast had needed to fuck me, to soothe it and end the fever. Angh had needed to bury himself in me, to spend his seed in me to know that he'd marked me as his. That I was truly claimed.

Now, I was his. The cuffs about our wrists proved it. His beast didn't need reassurance. Angh didn't need to prove to the universe that I belonged to him. It was just us now. Kira and Angh. Lovers. Mates. We could fuck any way we wanted. Fast. Slow. Hard. Gentle. Wild.

So while Angh had reassured himself and his beast that I was his, now I would take him. It was my turn to have my way with him, to know he belonged to me, that his huge beast cock was mine to use as I saw fit.

And I wanted it to fit deep in my wet pussy. Now.

"It's time for your test, Warlord."

When I put one knee on the bed beside his hip, he moved his hand away from the base of his cock. When I settled my other knee and I was straddling him, he held his breath. When I hovered over him, the tip of his cock nudging my entrance, I met his gaze. Held it.

And when I lowered myself down, took him into me, deeper and deeper still, we groaned. I had to shimmy my hips to get him to fit, but I was ready for him. I'd been ready since the brig.

It took some time, but I finally sat upon his lap, the backs of my thighs against his. The short hairs tickled my skin, but it was how deep he was, the way he filled me that had me catching my breath.

I watched as his jaw clenched, sweat beaded on his brow. His hands gripped the bedding by his hips, most likely with an effort not to touch me, to take over.

I lifted up, then dropped back down. Again. Then again.

My hands went to his shoulders and I held on as my need took over. I couldn't go slow any longer. It was impossible with the way I felt. I was chasing my orgasm each time I settled on him, ground my hips and my clit against him. The wet sounds of fucking filled the room. Our breaths mingled. I pushed him and he fell back onto his elbows, propped up and watching. I had room to move now, to ride him like a dang cowgirl.

I closed my eyes, cupped my breasts and rode him.

"Angh! Yes, god yes. I'm going to come. Your cock, god it's...oh my—"

My mind went blank the more I rode him, the faster he stroked every perfect place inside me.

"Touch me," I commanded and a second later, my hands were pushed away from my breasts as his big hand touched them both. A finger brushed over my clit and my eyes flew open.

I looked at him as I came. As I screamed my pleasure. As I milked the cum from his balls. He groaned, stiffened and I felt the thick spurts as he filled me up.

When I finally caught my breath, I told him, "You passed."

He took my hand, tugged me down on top of him for a kiss, then rolled us so he was looming over me, his cock still buried deep. He grinned, stroked my cheek.

"The test isn't over yet, *mate*."

EPILOGUE

A̶ngh, Sector 437, Battleship Karter, Two Weeks Later

"Mommy!" a little girl shouted, hopping up and down as she ran through the opening in the sliding doors toward Chloe. I wasn't sure how the little one's movement was possible, but being almost two, she could wiggle and squirm in the strangest of ways.

Chloe dropped to her knees and opened her arms, the child being pulled into a hug and lots of kisses.

I smiled. Yes. I actually smiled.

It was good to see my friend be so happy, to watch her with her family. Chloe had mates who loved her, children. Dorian had been on the mission with us as a pilot. While his role was specific and kept him in his shuttle, he'd done an excellent job monitoring his mate as she worked. He had retired when Dara was born, but the Coalition needed him. When Commander Karter asked for his help, he couldn't refuse, nor did he wish to. Especially when serving the Fleet once more meant he could help keep his mate safe on her I.C. missions.

I could only imagine how hard it was for him to watch her leave his side; the idea of Kira having gone on so many dangerous missions without me made me panic, even though there was nothing I could do about events that had already happened.

But now? Now she was by my side. I glanced to her, watched her watching Chloe. Seth came through the sliding door of the meeting room seconds behind his daughter, our debriefing session just wrapping up.

We'd done it. Destroyed the Hive minefield that had held the Battleship Karter in a deadlock for the last few months. Kira and I could hear the hidden Nexus nodes, the A.I. centerpieces of the Hive weapon. And when we were with Chloe, the combined effect of all three of our brain implants amplified everything until it was like the control nodes practically announced their locations. Begged me to destroy them.

I was only too happy to comply.

Our celebration would last a few hours at most. We'd already been contacted by Vice Admiral Niobe and informed that the I.C. was now working on a schedule of missions that would send Kira and I all over the galaxy to take out the webs of mines. But the I.C. needed a couple of days to decide where to strike first.

They never went in without a plan. Kira and I were warriors. We would go where they sent us. Together.

Most of the crew who had been part of this mission had left the debriefing room nearly half an hour earlier, heading to the showers, their living quarters to see their mates, to the cafeteria or even the canteen for drinks. Anything to unwind before being called up again for another mission.

Only a handful of us remained, Chloe and Dorian, Kira and myself. That was, until the door slid open and Seth walked in right behind his daughter, his new infant son, Christopher, safely cuddled up on the warrior's shoulder.

Seth's big hand patted the tiny back. I couldn't tell if the baby was asleep yet from where I stood, but he had golden hair and caramel colored skin like Dorian. The baby's features were sharper than Seth's, an obvious sign of his Prillon parentage, but the green eyes were pure Chloe. They had named the little one in honor of Seth's brother, Christopher, who had been killed in battle with the Hive. The tiny boy's hair stuck up every which way. Their little girl, Dara, had black hair like her mother and her mother's green eyes. She was definitely human and Seth's biological child. Not that it mattered. The golden collars about the three mates' necks made them a family. Which mate's seed created the child was irrelevant as long as he or she was loved. And with this family, they were so very loved.

"Did you have fun with Daddy while we were gone?" Chloe asked, referring to Seth. I'd learned quickly that Seth was *Daddy* and Dorian was *Papa*. Earth terms of endearment that I would, someday, gods willing, hear from my own beautiful little girl's lips. Mine and Kira's.

Dara nodded, but her curious green eyes turned to me. "Can I fly again?" she asked, her voice loud for one so tiny.

The last time I'd seen her, she'd been brave enough to come over to me and comment on how tall I was. I'd lifted her into the air over my head and she'd squealed with delight. I'd smiled at her easy pleasure, so innocent.

I crossed my arms over my chest and gave her a mock stern look. "Did you eat all of your vegetables at breakfast?"

She laughed. "Silly Warlord, there aren't any vegbles in my breakfast."

I bent down and held my hands out. "Then I guess you can fly."

Not a fearful bone in her little body, she launched herself into my hold and I tossed her up in the air. All three of her parents gasped and stepped toward me, but I would not allow a single hair on her head to be harmed. She laughed and giggled when I caught her. "Again!"

"Wait until you have one of your own and you'll have a heart attack over everything," Chloe said to Kira.

Kira looked at her, the stillness in my mate's body making me pay attention. "Why did you stay? When Commander Karter asked you to keep fighting? You told the Vice Admiral that you were going to retire to Prillon Prime but chose not to. You have children now. The risk, it's terrifying. So why did you stay?"

Chloe looked from my mate to her daughter, more love than I'd ever seen on her face shining from her eyes. "The new Hive weapon could destroy everything, Kira. If we don't destroy them, there won't be anywhere my babies would be safe. No starship. No planet, no matter how far away. I couldn't live with that threat hanging over their heads, not when I could do something about it. Do you understand?"

Kira's hand settled over her lower stomach and I

imagined our child growing there. When her gaze lifted to mine, I knew she was thinking the exact same thing.

"Yes, and I admire your courage. Yours and your mates'. Someday, I want children, and I want them to have a chance to grow up happy. Safe. But for now, I have a huge Atlan beast to supervise."

I tucked Dara against my side as I looked to Chloe. "Supervise? Woman, who's the one who went off on secret missions without her mate?"

Kira rolled her eyes at me as Seth chuckled. "Warlord, you and your beast need to have a little powwow. I know you haven't been mated long, so let me give you a little advice. Earth women don't like to be reminded of their past mistakes. Or any mistakes, for that matter."

I frowned and saw that Kira *and* Chloe had their arms crossed over their chests, eyes narrowed.

"What is a powwow?" I asked.

Kira and Chloe looked at each other and I glanced at Dorian, who shrugged. "Out of all that, the thing you misunderstood was powwow?"

"Do I look like I'm from Earth?"

Dara's little hand patted my cheek. "You're big. You're from Atlan!" she said, pleased with herself.

The door slid open and the commander came in. "Uh oh," he said, looking at the women, then at Dara. "What did your daddy do this time?"

Dara squealed and reached for him, squirming like a worm in my hold. With a chuckle, I gently handed the precious bundle to Commander Karter, who immediately took hold of her ankles and spun her in circles as she screamed to go faster.

Chloe groaned, her forehead landing in her palm. "Oh my god, she's an adrenaline junkie already."

Kira laughed, the sound one I rarely heard from her, a deep belly laugh filled with pure joy. "That's it. I'm not having babies. I'd be too terrified."

When Karter was done, he lifted Dara to his shoulders where she made a dramatic display of swirling her head around on her neck like she was dizzy. Karter held her safely in place and looked at Seth again. "Well?"

Seth patted the baby's bottom and laughed. "Me? I didn't do anything. I *know* Earth women. It wasn't me."

Dorian held up his hands when the commander turned to him. "Nope. I *know* one Earth woman and trust me, I learned my lessons about crossing her a long time ago."

"That leaves you, Atlan." Commander Karter looked to me. "Sounds like you need some time with your mate, Warlord, to learn how to handle your human female."

"You could use some leave yourself, Commander," Chloe added.

Karter gave her a quick glance but ignored her *and* her comment. Obviously, the commander didn't agree, even though he worked as hard, if not harder, than anyone else. He might not go out on missions, but it was his duty to send them out there to face death.

"Captain Dahl."

"Yes, sir?" Kira asked.

"Take your Atlan beast to guest quarters. You're on leave for forty-eight hours. I will inform the Vice Admiral that I need you for a bit longer. It seems you two haven't gotten to know each other well enough. Yet."

Kira was trying not to smile, but said, "Yes, sir."

Dorian took the baby from Seth. The love in his eyes transformed him from a warrior to a father in an instant. "Give me the baby. You've had our family all to yourself for hours."

"Not Mommy." Seth pulled Chloe in for a kiss as Dara bounced up and down on Commander Karter's shoulders clapping and chanting. "Mommy, Mommy, Mommy."

Confused, I looked around at all the goofy, sappy eyed expressions on the warriors faces. My beast was rumbling as well, feeling uncomfortable with all of the...*togetherness*. "Is this a powwow?"

Kira took one look at me and smiled. "Come on, mate. It seems I have some things to teach you."

Based on the sly smile on her face as she took my hand and led me out the room, I had a feeling what she was saying aloud and what she meant were two different things.

Once we were out in the hall away from the others— and little ears— I stopped and she turned around to face me. I leaned down, stroked her cheek. "What kinds of things do you have to teach me?" My voice was dipped low, and my tone was dark. I was thinking about all kinds of things I wanted to teach her, naked. In bed. Up against the wall. In the bath... My beast perked up and wanted to hear the answer as well.

She continued to smile. "I'm the Academy instructor here, Atlan. While I might not be ready for children yet, we should certainly practice."

My cock perked up at that. Fuck, yes, we could practice.

"I will teach you about Earth traditions."

"What kind of traditions?"

Her eyes grew dark, her cheeks turning pink, and I knew whatever she was going to say, I wanted to hear it. "Ever heard of the reverse cowgirl?"

"No." I traced her bottom lip with my finger just so I could feel the heat of her breath on my flesh. "What is this reverse cowgirl?"

She nipped at the tip of my finger, then sucked it into her mouth in a blatant imitation of what she'd done to my cock on previous occasions. "Just one sexual position that we Earth females usually like."

The beast growled, there was no stopping him. "There are others?"

"Oh, yes."

I leaned in even further. "As long as you're riding my cock, I will be your very best student."

She grabbed my hand and tugged, pulling me down the hall. I let her lead because wherever she went, I would follow. Forever.

Mine.

For once, the beast and I were in complete and total agreement.

A SPECIAL THANK YOU TO MY READERS...

Want more? I've got **hidden** bonus content on my web
site *exclusively* for those on my <u>mailing list.</u>

If you are already on my email list, you don't need to do a thing!
Simply scroll to the bottom of my newsletter emails and click on
the *super-secret* link.

Not a member? What are you waiting for? In addition to ALL of
my bonus content (great new stuff will be added regularly) you
will be the first to hear about my newest release the second it
hits the stores—AND you will get a free book as a special
welcome gift.

Sign up now! http://freescifiromance.com

FIND YOUR INTERSTELLAR MATCH!

YOUR mate is out there. Take the test today and discover your perfect match. Are you ready for a sexy alien mate (or two)?

VOLUNTEER NOW!

interstellarbridesprogram.com

DO YOU LOVE AUDIOBOOKS?

Grace Goodwin's books are now available as
audiobooks...everywhere.

LET'S TALK SPOILER ROOM!

Interested in joining my **Sci-Fi Squad**? Meet new like-minded sci-fi romance fanatics and chat with Grace! Get excerpts, cover reveals and sneak peeks before anyone else. Be part of a private Facebook group that shares pictures and fun news! Join here:

https://www.facebook.com/groups/scifisquad/

***

Want to talk about Grace Goodwin books with others? Join the **SPOILER ROOM** and spoil away! Your GG BFFs are waiting! (And so is Grace)

Join here:

https://www.facebook.com/groups/ggspoilerroom/

GET A FREE BOOK!

Join my mailing list to be the first to know of new releases, free books, special prices and other author giveaways.

http://freescifiromance.com

ALSO BY GRACE GOODWIN

Interstellar Brides® Program

Mastered by Her Mates

Assigned a Mate

Mated to the Warriors

Claimed by Her Mates

Taken by Her Mates

Mated to the Beast

Tamed by the Beast

Mated to the Vikens

Her Mate's Secret Baby

Mating Fever

Her Viken Mates

Fighting For Their Mate

Her Rogue Mates

Claimed By The Vikens

The Commanders' Mate

Matched and Mated

Hunted

Viken Command

Interstellar Brides® Program: The Colony

Surrender to the Cyborgs

Mated to the Cyborgs

Cyborg Seduction

Her Cyborg Beast

Cyborg Fever

Rogue Cyborg

Cyborg's Secret Baby

Interstellar Brides® Program: The Virgins

The Alien's Mate

Claiming His Virgin

His Virgin Mate

His Virgin Bride

Interstellar Brides® Program: Ascension Saga

Ascension Saga, book 1

Ascension Saga, book 2

Ascension Saga, book 3

Trinity: Ascension Saga - Volume 1

Ascension Saga, book 4

Ascension Saga, book 5

Ascension Saga, book 6

Faith: Ascension Saga - Volume 2

Ascension Saga, book 7

Ascension Saga, book 8

Ascension Saga, book 9

Destiny: Ascension Saga - Volume 3

Other Books

Their Conquered Bride

Wild Wolf Claiming: A Howl's Romance

ABOUT GRACE

Grace Goodwin is a *USA Today* and international bestselling author of Sci-Fi & Paranormal romance. Grace believes all women should be treated like royalty, in the bedroom and out of it, and writes love stories where men know how to make their women feel pampered, protected and very well taken care of. Grace hates the snow, loves the mountains (yes, that's a problem) and wishes she could simply download the stories out of her head instead of being forced to type them out. Grace lives in the western US and is a full-time writer, an avid reader and an admitted caffeine addict. She is active on Facebook and loves to chat with readers and fellow sci-fi fanatics.

All of Grace's books can be read as sexy, stand-alone adventures. But be careful, she likes her heroes hot and her love scenes hotter. You have been warned...

www.gracegoodwin.com
gracegoodwinauthor@gmail.com

Lightning Source UK Ltd.
Milton Keynes UK
UKHW021836210221
379147UK00005B/668